THE ADVENTURES OF
KATIE AND ASHLEY
BOOK ONE

MIRACLES CAN HAPPEN

THE RING

CARYN LESLEY

Order this book online at www.trafford.com
or email orders@trafford.com

Most Trafford titles are also available at major online book retailers.

Printed in the United States of America.

ISBN: 978-1-4669-1421-6 (sc)
ISBN: 978-1-4669-1422-3 (e)

Library of Congress Control Number: 2012903177

Trafford rev. 02/27/2012

 www.trafford.com

North America & international
toll-free: 1 888 232 4444 (USA & Canada)
phone: 250 383 6864 ♦ fax: 812 355 4082

CONTENTS

ACKNOWLEDGEMENTS

As always, there are many people who help make an author's words became reality in the form of a book.

I would like to thank my husband Michael for always being there while I was glued to my computer, and for the encouragement he offered to help me create Katie and Ashley's story.

I would like to thank my editor, Alice Eachus, for her never-ending support, her ease with words, and her literary abilities. I was blessed to have her work with me to enhance my book. My illustrator Peggy Dressel made Miracles Can Happen come to life. I want to thank her for the beautiful job she did on the cover.

I would also like to thank my eleven-year-old reader, Ava Buchwald, whose comments I have taken to heart. Because of her enthusiasm for Katie and Ashley's adventures, I've been encouraged to continue the series. Ava claimed she couldn't put the book down, and now can't wait to pick up the next adventure. What a thrill for an author! And no one *made* her say it. Even better!

Miracles Can Happen: The Ring was such fun to write, and I hope you enjoy it as much as I did writing it.

DEDICATION

I joyfully dedicate *Miracles Can Happen: The Ring* to my grandchildren, Reed, Spencer, Gavin, Brady, and Grace. I hope they each find their passion and experience it to the fullest every day of their lives.

I have found mine.

PROLOGUE

As Angelina nestled deep in her cracked leather seat on the train to somewhere, she watched the countryside dance and jump like scenes from a child's kaleidoscope. Trees were as bare as skeletons with forked limbs reaching high into the cold blue sky begging for the warmth of the sun. The rolling hills blended shades of yellow, brown, and black, their crops harvested long before with only straggled husks to remember the summer season.

Captured in her cozy compartment, well protected from the harshness of the passing scene, Angelina sensed the air outside had chilled more than expected. She pulled her pearl-buttoned, rose-hued sweater close and wrapped it around her tiny frame to protect herself from the bitter cold.

Another mission, another place, and so much to prepare! Angelina was tired, so very tired, but she was on an assignment and could not rest just yet. In a few hours she would leave the train and get ready to start her important mission. This time she would open a store. Not for the first time, mind you, but this special store was set to open very soon and there was still so much to do before customers could be welcomed. Angelina was running much later than she should be, and that worried her.

The tiny lady sighed and closed her eyes, hoping a few moments of sleep would bless her before the train pulled into the city that she would call her home.

CHAPTER ONE

Let the Adventure Begin

Katie Richards was all of twelve years old. She had brilliant blue eyes the color of the sea and beautiful golden hair weaving softly to her waist. She lived with her mother Amanda in a tiny, but charming apartment. The walls were rosy beige and pictures Amanda had painted when she was a young girl sprinkled every wall. Flowers and gardens were her favorite subjects to paint and now they charmed autumn's chill away.

Katie thought some of the paintings were a little weird, but her mom insisted that's how *she* saw flowers and beauty was *always* in the eye of the beholder. Whatever. They did add a riot of color, that was for sure!

Katie's father died when she was only three. She remembered her daddy as tall and slim with a face that always carried a smile. He would give Katie big bear hugs and toss her high in the air when he walked through the door each night. Swirling, twirling, and whirling, little Katie always choreographed a welcome dance for her daddy, sometimes waltzing with Pooh the Bear, Wally the Walrus or Miss Raggedy Ann Rosie to the silly sounds of *Sesame Street*.

Her daddy would smother her with kisses, tell her how much he loved her in a deep, deep growl and swing her round and round until she was hopelessly dizzy. Katie absolutely adored him. Now when she thought how much she missed this daddy she hardly knew, tears would flood her big blue eyes. Why did he have to be killed anyway?

Amanda was a hard-working woman, and Katie knew it even though she didn't always appreciate her efforts. Amanda worked as a waitress at The Cozy Corner, a popular mom and pop diner on the street where the Richards lived. She took double shifts sometimes to make ends meet or to buy something special. Money was always tight, but this proud mother and daughter were doing just fine, thank you very much.

Katie liked to stop by "The Cozy" to visit her mom on the way home from school and often warmed up with an on-the-house hot chocolate stuffed with marshmallows offered by Herb, her mom's boss.

With her mom's hectic schedule Katie was left alone much of the time, especially on the weekends, but she made the best of it.

Katie tried to help her mom with the housework and cooking so they'd have more time to play when they did have hours to spend together, but she had problems, plenty of problems, when she debuted in her young Martha Stewart role.

The first time Katie tried to run the washing machine, she added way too much detergent, forcing a frenzy of froth that created a blanket of bubbles reaching from the kitchen to the front door. "Katie the Creative" to the rescue! Grabbing a rusty snow shovel from the hall closet, the Martha wannabe spent an hour scooping suds and flinging them over the fire escape, much to the delight of the squealing toddlers and barking dogs below.

Learning a valuable lesson, Katie measured soap flakes like a mad scientist from then on, but became quite the pop artiste as carelessly sorted clothing became almost psychedelic after a spin in the old Maytag machine. Katie's brighty-whitey undies often turned into baby blues after doing battle with an army of navy towels. The towels won of course, spilling their blue blood over everything they conquered.

But, Katie learned, and churned, and finally mastered the Maytag!

Vacuuming encouraged Katie's personal work-out routine. Up, down, lunge, squat—all her muscle groups were worked, and worked hard. The Richards' rugs were clean enough to sleep on. Who said housework wasn't *really* a form of exercise!

But, cooking, ah cooking, was Katie's true passion! The Food Network replaced MTV as Must-See-TV and Katie's go-to recipe box quickly grew. She loved to try recipes offered on the backs of packages, assuming a food company would never print a recipe that turned out yucky. What would be the point of that?

From her early offerings of pigs-in-a-blanket and variations on the Manwich theme, Katie, the pint-sized domestic goddess, was soon sautéing, grilling, flambéing and roasting with the best of them. Unintended bites of cayenne once kept Katie and Amanda up all night jumping like Mexican beans. Lesson learned.

All domestic shenanigans were witnessed by Max, a big ol' calico cat trimmed in shades of yellow and tan. Max was the purr-fect companion. He was smart, affectionate and gifted with discriminating taste buds. Max always knew when to keep his mouth shut, and was never known to blab a secret. Katie found Max behind a dumpster years before and he quickly became the man of the house.

Katie had her own room which she painted a sunny apricot all by herself. It wasn't a big room, but big enough to hold a bed draped in fluffy white chenille with moss green pillows holding court. Stacks of beige canvas bins held clothes, and a white wicker desk was crowned with a clunky computer Amanda found in the newspaper want-ads. Dozens of interesting purple and green bottles lined the window sills, all filled with plant cuttings resembling modern art.

Katie loved her room! Sitting cross-legged on her bed was the best place to do homework and just a quick slouch down offered a comfortable place to chat with Emily, her very best friend since she was five-years-old.

Posters of Justin Bieber plastered Katie's walls; he was her absolutely fav guy in the whole world and Katie just couldn't read enough about him. Most of her conversations with Emily started with, "If Justin called you, would you believe it was really him?"

On her way home from school one Tuesday, Katie couldn't stop thinking about the "OMG—Can You Believe It's Justin" concert Emily invited her to attend. Emily was turning thirteen, and was allowed to invite a few friends to celebrate her first teen birthday.

Emily's parents were members of a county club on Long Island where they would be having dinner before the concert. But, who could possibly eat! Emily's parents arranged for a limo to take the party girls to the concert where they scored front row seats. This party was just going to be too cool! Katie was freaking out at just the thought of it all. Em's dad Joe worked for Virgin Records and copped the concert tickets—how great was that!

Best of all, Emily's dad arranged for them to actually meet Justin and get autographs. Katie adored Emily's family, especially her sister Allie, and knew Em's parents would make this one night to remember forever. The girls just couldn't stop talking about how cool this whole birthday would be!

This would be Katie's first grown-up party at a country club, and to have Justin Bieber as the main attraction was just too much. But Katie worried she would have to say no to the invitation, and she couldn't bear the thought of it. She had nothing to wear and all the other girls would be dressed to kill. There just wasn't enough money in the household budget for a cool outfit this month. When the fridge went out last week, any extra money went for repairs. Katie just didn't feel right asking her mom to splurge on her right now. She wanted to give Emily a wonderful birthday present and that would eat up all the money she had saved.

Sometimes Katie felt very left out of things. *If only I could go and have fun like everyone else, just for one night,* she murmured to herself as she walked slowly down the street heading for home.

Usually Katie rushed home from school to play with Max whose antics always made her laugh, but today she just wasn't up to it. As she passed the familiar stores, Katie threw an unannounced pity party for herself and each step made her more miserable.

Katie was a block from home when she noticed a storefront window that she swore was empty just the day before. The window was now overwhelmed with splashes of color that couldn't possibly go unnoticed.

With a gasp, Katie saw an incredibly cool deep pink skirt topped with an outrageous tie-dyed cami in shades of purple and pink draped over a headless mannequin. Over the cami was the neatest jean jacket in soft pink with rows of rhinestones speckling the breast pockets. OMG—it was unreal! This was exactly the outfit Katie always imagined wearing to her first big party!

Wow, Katie thought to herself, *this is the most awesome outfit I've ever seen!* She decided to investigate what the new shop had to offer, but knew she would never be able to afford the high-end outfit. With a sense of urgency, something deep inside whispered, *It won't cost anything to try it on!*

Out of nowhere, a little old lady popped her head around a display and warmly welcomed Katie to the store.

"Welcome to *Miracles Can Happen,* my dear. My name is Angelina. I'm so glad you stopped by."

Katie immediately thought Angelina resembled a pixie with a bowl of wispy white hair framing her small wrinkled face. Angelina was just like Katie pictured her grandmother would look if she were still living.

The little pixie was elegantly dressed in a white suit with a single strand of pearls draped around her neck. Her tiny feet wore silver velvet slippers with rhinestone crystals scattered over them. Her ears were pierced with pearl and diamond earrings that made her violet eyes sparkle. She had a rosy glow about her, and a definite twinkle in her eye.

Katie glanced in awe at the shop's white wicker shelves climbing from floor to ceiling, all filled with pastel sweaters folded neatly in rows with hundreds of delicate accessories marching along beside them.

Miracles Can Happen resembled a scene from an old-fashioned fairytale. It was totally outrageous! Walls were covered in pink and white flowered wallpaper that mercifully toned down the hot bubble-gum carpeting. This was like living in a world of cotton candy!

Lace curtains covered the shop's sparkling windows as tiny lights winked from the ceiling like stars in the night sky.

The three dressing rooms were hidden behind billows of lavender organza and the white clouds painted above them looked like memories of a summer day. Fresh flowers gathered casually in ornate silver urns were perched everywhere. The shop smelled like a flower garden in full bloom. This was certainly nothing like Old Navy!

"How can I help you today, dear, and what's your name?" Angelina asked with a smile that welcomed response.

Surprising herself, Katie replied confidently, "Oh, my name is Katie and I would love to try on the outrageous outfit in the window. Do you think I could?"

"Certainly you can, dear Katie," Angelina crooned as she headed to the window. "I believe the top and skirt are just your size. Let me take them down for you, it will only be a minute. You can try the skirt and cami with the jacket, what do you think?"

Katie called back, "Oh, yes, I just love the jacket too!"

While she waited, Katie curled down deep in an overstuffed ivory satin chair, marveling at all the fluff and stuff surrounding her in this strange boutique. What a find! Everything was absolutely defined to the last detail—even dresses were hung on lace hangers trimmed with pink ribbons. This little store sure wasn't like most shops she visited. Katie wasn't sure she liked it—it was just too weird.

"Here," Angelina offered, "Let's see how this looks on you."

The little lady guided Katie to the dressing area and gently parted the overdone curtains to offer a room that looked like a fairy princess fantasy. Her friends would really never, ever believe this! Katie wondered if she would even admit she visited such a strange place and worse yet, stayed!

Shuddering as if suddenly cold, an odd feeling enveloped Katie as she discovered she was beginning to enjoy the little store and the gentle Angelina. What in the world was happening to her?

In a corner, Katie spied a wicker table piled high with iced cupcakes topped with frosted pink roses. The cupcakes were arranged in tiers on scalloped china servers with sprigs of rosemary peeking around the delicate offerings. A silver tray held a crystal pitcher of pink lemonade teased with mint standing ready to be poured into a collection of crystal goblets. This was just too, too much to be believed. Katie wondered if she was falling under some strange spell.

The dressing room was enormous with floor to ceiling mirrors on three sides. Katie could see herself from every angle. An elevated stage was centered in the middle of the dressing area for optimal views. This was so cool!

"Katie, please let me know when you're ready and we'll see what you look like," Angelina called over her shoulder as she left the room.

Katie slipped off her navy skirt and yellow blouse and let them drop to the floor in a puddle. Ever so carefully she lifted the exquisite pink satin skirt from its hanger. The fabric was layered with pleats and tucks in unusual places. Katie wasn't exactly sure how the skirt should fit, but she loved the feel of it against her skin.

Lifting her arms to let the skirt surround her, Katie closed her eyes and pictured herself at the concert with her friends. Slowly she slipped the cami in place. The tie-dyed pattern of palest pink and bright purple was so hot, especially with iridescent rhinestones blinking as she moved. Katie was positive this was the most epic outfit ever! Then she put on the jacket, the absolute finishing touch. Katie was amazed how perfectly every piece fit.

"I'm ready," Katie called to Angelina. She kept her eyes tightly closed. Katie didn't want to break the fantasy playing in her mind, particularly now that Justin had just reached for her hand!

Angelina appeared without a sound, and her eyes sparkled when she saw Katie.

"This was made just for you! Everything fits so well and you look amazing," Angelina gushed. The little shopkeeper thought the tiny twinkling stones on the cami reflected the happiness on young Katie's face.

Still facing the curtains to block her view, Katie loosened her rubber-banded ponytail. She was almost afraid to turn to face her reflection. Looking in the glass would harshly remind her that this outrageous outfit could never be hers.

Taking a deep breath, Katie turned to face the walls covered with mirrors, feeling Angelina's eyes leading her. Wanting just a quick peek, Katie's eyes flew open wide when she saw her image. OMG! She looked *really* good! Katie wanted so much to own this explosive outfit, but she knew it would take a genuine miracle for *that* to happen. Coming in here *was* a big mistake! It only made her feel worse.

"Well," asked Angelina hopefully, "what do you think?"

"Oh," sighed Katie. "I just love it, but I must bring my mother to your shop for her opinion."

Katie knew they could never afford this extravagant purchase, but she couldn't bring herself to tell the nice lady the truth.

"Certainly, I understand. I'll put it in the back and hold it for you until tomorrow afternoon. What is your last name, my dear?"

"Richards, Katie Richards."

"Why Katie, that's a beautiful name!" replied Angelina, making notes on a pink hold tag.

Good grief! Would this "everything pink" stuff never end Katie wondered as she turned to leave.

Once out of Angelina's sight, Katie practically danced as she headed for home. She saw herself wearing the amazing outfit at Em's party.

When she reached her front door, hard reality hit and Katie realized her dream was just that, a dream. How would her mom ever be able to get the money for something like this? Katie opened the door with her key and found faithful Max there to greet her. After smothering the tears rolling down her cheeks in Max's soft fur, Katie busied herself with her chores for the day.

No second shift at the restaurant tonight, Katie remembered. She was happy about that because she wanted to share her day's excitement with her mom. Katie tried to be careful not to make her mother feel bad because they couldn't afford many luxuries, but sometimes it was hard to hold her feelings in.

Katie set the table with their one extravagance, her grandmother's elegant antique silver. The night before, Amanda and Katie cooked together and concocted a killer chicken soup recipe. Katie put the kettle of chicken with vegetables soup on the stove and began tearing romaine lettuce for a simple salad.

Chores finished, Katie sat down at her desk and booted her computer to begin her homework research, and check Justin's Twitter account, of course!

CHAPTER TWO

Rhinestones and Satin

Katie's mom was a beautiful woman. Boy was she beautiful! Sometimes Katie felt a smidge jealous when even the boys *her* age fell all over themselves trying to flirt with her. What was that all about? What weirdos!

Amanda rarely wore make-up, she simply didn't need to. Besides that, Amanda hardly had the money or the time to spend pampering herself at a spa or salon. On the other hand, Katie loved to blow her allowance on every flavored lip gloss or metallic polish she could find at the CVS or Walgreen's.

As a young widow, Amanda had no choice but to work to pay the rent and take care of her young daughter. Her parents had passed away many years before and she had no brothers or sisters. Her husband was an only child too and his parents were gone, so Amanda was completely, absolutely, totally on her own.

Holidays were bad, really bad, with nobody to sit around the Richards' table to make merry. Thank goodness Emily's parents always invited Amanda and Katie to join them as part of their family, which seemed to number in the hundreds anyway. Emily loved to introduce Katie as a far removed relative on a lost side of the family, which elevated Katie to instant star status.

Most of the time, life at the Richards' house was the same old-same old routine. Amanda and Katie simply did what they had to do.

The Cozy Corner was the perfect place for Amanda to work. She'd waitressed there for eight years and embraced her customers like old friends. In turn, Katie was "adopted" as a favorite grandkid or niece. Talk about being spoiled—it worked for her!

Amanda was always on time for work, never complained, and everybody adored her. The best part was that the diner was only a few minutes from the apartment so a car wasn't needed. With the New York subway only a block away, there was never a problem getting around the city. Life was good, even on a budget.

When she was a little kid, Katie spent her time in day care under the watchful eye of stern Miss Sylvia, but when she finally started kindergarten, Katie held court at The Cozy after school. Her crayon pictures shouted their colors at every booth, and the five-year-old Ms. Picasso's interpretation of a stack of pancakes was copied, laminated, and welcomed early-birds to the breakfast menu.

When she reached the age when Amanda felt Max could take over the role of after-school supervisor, Katie would rush home from school, double-step the stairs, unlock the door and settle in for an afternoon of homework . . . after calling Em to gossip about what went on at school that day.

This year there were two new guys in their class who'd moved from the Midwest over the summer and the two were the main topic of conversation most days. One was dark and looked like a very young Johnny Depp, but wore a sneer that was wickedly captivating. The other guy looked like a freaked out surfer and nobody could figure out how the great state of Kansas could possibly produce such an all right dude.

As Amanda walked through the door on that Tuesday night, aromas from the soup they'd whipped up Monday night welcomed her. She could tell Katie had modified the recipe that afternoon when fresh herbs tickled her nose. Her young Martha Stewart was just pulling cheese toast from the oven when Amanda arrived.

For being only twelve, Amanda thought, Katie was really special and very creative in the kitchen. Katie was a good kid, and Amanda wished she could do more for her as she watched her culinary intense daughter pull the bread from the oven.

"Hi darlin', I'm home, how was your day?" Amanda called out.

"Okay, Mom, I guess. How was yours?"

Max was there with the same greeting he gave every night—a long slink around Amanda's ankles. That cat had to have some reptile in his genes!

"Oh, nothing new or exciting," Amanda sighed. Dropping her coat on a chair, she walked to the kitchen sink and washed the day's work from her hands.

Katie finished setting the table, carefully placing the ivory linen napkins handed down from her grandmother next to the heavy silverware. It always surprised her how good a simple meal tasted when the table looked great.

Well, the Food Network always preached presentation was everything; maybe they've got something there, Katie mused as she placed a glass bottle of trailing ivy in the center of the table.

Amanda was relieved to enjoy a night off. She hated leaving Katie alone for such a long time every day and getting home early was a welcome change. With the days growing shorter, Amanda knew dinner traffic at the restaurant would pick up soon and double shifts would happen most every day.

"Dinner is ready, Mom. Have a seat and relax. This time I'll wait on *you* for a change! Do you think you could handle that?" Katie teased.

"Oh, I can give it a good try! Katie, this soup is really fantastic. What did you add to it?" Amanda asked.

"Not much, just a little tarragon to bring out the chicken flavor. You know, Mom, together we could have our own TV show I bet. We could call it *Mama and her Munchkin*! I bet it would be a real hit."

Laughing, the mother and daughter gobbled down the chicken soup, chockfull of beans, okra, cabbage, onions, zucchini and big chunks of chicken.

As they were sopping soup from the bottom of their bowls, Amanda noticed Katie had became very quiet and looked worried.

"Katie, what's wrong? Are you feeling okay?"

"Well, I guess I do feel kinda bad. Emily is having this unreal birthday bash. Her parents invited eight kids to their country club for dinner—and I'm glad you're sitting down, Mom, because this will blow you away with its coolness—after dinner, a big limo is taking everybody to the Justin Beiber concert! Front row seats too, and Em's dad fixed it so the kids get to meet Justin in the flesh! All the kids are talking about the new outfits they're getting and I guess that leaves me out of the party. I have nothing to wear that's dressy enough.

"I'm sorry, Mom, I don't mean to upset you or be a whiner, but when I was walking home from school today I passed a new clothes store. It must have just opened because I never saw it before. The shop is a little weird, plenty weird actually, but right there in the window was an outfit that's just awesome! I went in and tried it on, just to see how I would look."

Katie went on and on about the funky rose satin skirt and the purple tie-dyed rhinestone top. Amanda grew quiet while her heart was breaking for her daughter.

"Katie, I'll tell you what. I'll take a late lunch tomorrow and meet you at the shop as soon as school is out." Amanda sighed, not knowing where all this might lead.

"Oh, Mom! Really?" Katie jumped up and hugged her mother wildly. Even Max got excited and chased his tail around the chair legs. He had no clue what he was celebrating, but took the hint from his mistresses, hoping food was involved somewhere, somehow.

"Yes, dear, do you know how much the outfit costs?"

Katie rolled on, playing the afternoon adventure to the hilt.

"Wait 'til you see the layers and layers that make up the skirt—it's like overlapping waves. The top is not just purple, it's tie-dyed with streaks of pink with gobs of sparkle stuff all over it. I know you'll love it, and it fits perfectly, and there's a pink denim jacket too!"

Suddenly Katie realized she never asked about the price, knowing that would have ruined everything. But now she worried she was dragging her mom to the shop for nothing. That little number had to cost hundreds of dollars and buying it was as much a fantasy as the shop seemed to be.

"Katie, Katie, slow down! I'll see it tomorrow. Just tell me where to meet you."

Katie described how the tiny store on Fifth and Main appeared out of nowhere, and overnight no less, yet it was filled with tons of clothes that were perfectly placed. She babbled on about all the pink frothy stuff and the sweet pixie lady named Angelina.

After fifteen minutes of non-stop yakking, Amanda finally said, "Okay, enough already. It's homework time, so just calm down for now. I'll clean up and feed Max. Go finish studying, take your shower, and hit the sack. I'll be in to say goodnight soon."

After the last dish was put away, Amanda stood in a corner of the living room and looked out at the traffic clogging the avenue. She started making a plan. Well, she thought, I do have a little money put aside for Christmas. I guess Christmas could come early this year, and I still do have plenty of time to make more tips to buy Katie a few things to put in her stocking.

The next day the hours dragged before the final school bell rang. Katie was so excited that she had a hard time concentrating on her classes and was just happy she didn't have any tests that day. She was dying to tell Em about the outfit, but didn't dare in case it was a lost cause. That would be too humiliating, even with Em. The girls chatted about the party every chance they got as the countdown to the big day started. Emily was so excited, and Katie was happy to see her friend be the center of attention.

When the bell finally rang, Katie ran down the steps and all the way to *Miracles Can Happen*. Amanda arrived just as they had planned. Katie could tell her mom was impressed with the little shop—it was just too perfect. Angelina welcomed them warmly and had the outfit waiting in the dressing room for Katie to model.

"Katie," Angelina said with a twinkle in her eye, "I forgot to tell you yesterday that ballet flats and a lavender heart-shaped bag come with the outfit. It's all included for the same price. I think the shoes will fit, let's see. Come, dear, try on this beautiful creation for your mother."

Angelina pulled the billowy organza curtains aside once again and the three walked into the over-the-top dressing room. After cupcakes were passed, Katie turned to the two adults and asked that they leave so she could surprise them when she changed into a pink and purple fashionista.

Before taking the outfit off its hanger, Katie gave into temptation and poured a glass of pink lemonade to wash down the second chocolate cupcake smothered with cherry icing she had enjoyed once alone. Katie had been too excited to eat much of her lunch and was now absolutely starving.

While Katie was in Fantasyland trying on the clothes, Amanda pulled Angelina to a far corner of the shop.

"Angelina, it is an amazing outfit, but how much is it all together?"

"This is a resale shop," Angelina began to explain. "This outfit was worn once and then was sent to us to resell. All the money goes to charity, my dear. It is a designer outfit and quite expensive. Usually it would sell for $350, even second-hand."

Amanda's heart sank, and she had to sit down.

"But," Angelina hurried on, "I have it priced at eighty-five dollars for everything."

While Angelina made her pitch, an eager smile brightened her pixie face.

Amanda stood up and looked directly at the little old lady. She had fifty dollars in her pocket, the start of her Christmas fund. Maybe Angelina would let her pay that now and collect the remaining thirty-five dollars the next week.

Swallowing her pride, she asked Angelina if that would work for her. If Katie really, really wanted this outfit, Amanda would try her best to work it out, even if she had to borrow money from her boss.

Before Angelina could answer, Katie made her grand entrance with gyrating dance moves—she looked like she could be on the Disney Channel! Angelina couldn't help herself, she had to smooth down the skirt and straighten the jacket so that the cami just peaked through. She was a born saleswoman for sure!

Katie twirled and whirled so her mom could see the outfit in action. The ballet flats did fit perfectly and she wrapped the purse across her front for effect. She looked sensational!

Amanda was amazed at how grown up her daughter looked, and how happy she was. "Katie, you look fantastic!"

"Really, Mom, tell me the truth. I think I love the pink and purple too much to know if it really works on me."

"I think you look great, and if you want it, it's yours!"

Katie jumped up and down, kissed her mom on a bounce, and then ran to hug Angelina.

Back in the dressing room, Katie carefully took off her new outfit and practically screamed out loud. This was the best day ever!

Angelina finally answered Amanda's question with a yes, and suggested they take everything home that day. She would trust them for the final payment later.

"I adore your daughter," Angelina gushed, "and I'm so happy she's happy!" The little pixie face glowed with excitement—this was Angelina's crowning moment!

"Mom, you're the best in the whole world. *I'm gonna meet Justin Bieber, I'm gonna meet Justin Bieber,*" Katie sang at the top of her lungs as she danced around *Miracles*.

Angelina and Amanda couldn't help but laugh at Katie's animated show—if she was like this at twelve, her teen years would be entirely too much!

———◦●◦———

As soon as she got home, Katie called Emily. This was way too exciting news to text. Placing the phone on her shoulder, Katie curled comfortably in the big brown recliner in the living room. Max sat proudly on Katie's lap and stared into her huge blue eyes. Somehow that big cat knew something was going on, and his wiggling whiskers signaled he hoped food was involved.

"Hi, Dr. Landis, is Emily there?"

"Sure Katie, hold on a minute. Please say hi to your mom for me. I haven't seen her for awhile."

"I will," Katie assured her, and then added, "My mom has been really busy at work." Knowing her hearing was about to be assaulted, Katie held the phone away from her ear.

"Em, it's Katie calling, come grab the phone."

Emily's mother was thrilled Katie was her daughter's best friend. The girls were so different, yet so much the same. Emily was visually the opposite of Katie. She had shoulder-length, dark straight hair and brown eyes as big as saucers with eyelashes long enough to trip over. The only similarity was both were growing up to be beautiful, inside and out.

She was happy the girls spent at least one night at the other's home every other weekend. There was nothing to worry about when they were together. Trying on make-up, polishing toes, and applying temp tattoos took up a lot of their time, but of course they would find time to talk about the boys in their class, especially the new guys.

Emily finally picked up the phone and settled back in a wicker chair, ready for a good long talk.

"Em, guess what—I can come to your party after all! I even got a new outfit and I'm so excited!"

Emily was aware of the hard time Katie and her mom had making ends meet and tried to include Katie in as many things as she could. She loved Katie very much and sometimes it made her feel bad when Katie was left out of things because she couldn't afford to do them.

Emily's parents adored Katie too and became a second family to her. Emily had offered to lend Katie something to wear to the party, but size-wise it wasn't going to work. Emily was much taller and nothing fit. Emily also knew Katie had a proud streak so she tried to find ways to help without making a big deal of things. She had been hoping something would happen so Katie could come. Now that she was, and Emily couldn't help but exclaim, "Katie, now I am *really* excited about my party! I want you to sit right next to me. Promise?"

"Of course, I will. I can't wait for you to see my awesome pink and purple get-up. Do you think I should put pink streaks in my hair?" Katie offered as the ultimate accessory.

"Uh, no, that would be overkill for sure," Emily advised.

Katie went on to describe the whole shopping adventure, beginning to end, giving particular attention to Angelina and the garishly pinky-pinky shop that seemed to pop out of nowhere.

The two went on for over an hour and, of course, Justin and the party were mentioned over and over again.

Emily's mom halted the gossip session when she announced dinner was on the table. The BFFs promised to touch base later that night; there was so much to talk about!

CHAPTER THREE

JB Makes the Party

Katie and Amanda had a great time shopping for the perfect gift for Emily the week before her party. They finally found one they knew she really wanted—the coolest bracelet with the initials ECL—Emily Carol Landis—engraved in a pop heart design. It was as delicate as Emily was, and Katie couldn't wait for her BFF to be surprised.

Gift wrapping the little box was the most fun. Katie chose glossy silver paper and added yards of curly bright pink ribbon cascading over the top to make a real statement. She fashioned a gift tag from an old greeting card and wrote: *To my BBF on her birthday. I hope this year will be the most fun ever! Love, Katie.* To add glitz and glitter, Katie glued dozens of rhinestones all over the silver paper—it was so awesome!

Emily Landis was a very lucky girl, most would agree.

Not only was she pretty, but her family had money to burn. Her father was an executive at Virgin Records and her mother was a practicing psychiatrist with her own TV show. Even with their luxurious lifestyle trappings, the Landis family was down to earth and practical. Emily and her sister Allie had plenty of chores to do to keep them well grounded.

Em's parents made it clear that having money one day was no guarantee it would be there the next. The Landis girls were taught everybody must work hard for what they have, and not to expect a charmed life to be served to them on a silver platter.

But Emily did love to shop—boy, did she love to hit the stores! Em learned to copy pricey designer outfits and create the same look by shopping the aisles of Target. Em was the ultimate fashionista, and could take a belt or scarf and sling and fling it around to make a simple outfit look totally hot instantly. On Saturdays, friends would follow Em to the mall, just to copy her ideas. She was *that* good!

One day Emily hoped to become a fashion designer and have her own boutique where she could pull together great looks for anybody who wandered in. *Accessorize, accessorize, accessorize* was her personal mall call.

Katie loved raiding Em's closet, but unfortunately, Emily was two inches taller than Katie so most of the raiding was limited to jewelry, scarves, belts and purses. But Katie wasn't complaining—Em's little touches jazzed things up a whole lot and did wonders for her sometimes too, too neutral classics.

All the girls going to the party couldn't wait to see what Emily was wearing. They knew whatever she chose, it would be one epic look! Emily Lansing did seem to have it all—besides being pretty with fabulous taste, she was smart. She breezed through math and science with the highest marks, but her passion was English, particularly creative writing. Em hoped to write mystery novels with fashion as part of the plot. She kept a red leather notebook always handy to jot down ideas as they came to her. For the past few weeks, Em had been working on a short story that her teacher planned to send to the annual state-wide middle school writing contest. One more star for this girl!

School and homework were forgotten and placed far out of sight and far out of mind when Friday finally arrived. It had been a long week for the girls, and now the birthday party could officially begin.

Katie had been getting ready ever since she flew in the door after school let out. Max sensed something big was happening and was never more than an ankle-width away from his mistress, again hoping treats were part of the big event. No wonder he was so fat!

Amanda left work early to share Katie's excitement, keep her somewhat calm, and finally braid her daughter's long blond hair. This was going to be a night to remember for everybody.

Katie really rocked in her outfit. Amanda brushed a tear away when she realized her little girl was growing up, but tried not to put this sentiment into words knowing it would lead to typical tween eye rolling if she did. So, Amanda just smiled and complimented Katie with the words *cool, awesome* and *outrageous.*

As Katie was putting on pink lip gloss and a smidgen of blush, Amanda remembered a silver bracelet she had stuffed in the back of her top dresser drawer. It would be the perfect thing to bring out the flash of the rhinestones. After polishing it to a shine with a yellow kitchen towel, Amanda slipped it on Katie's tiny wrist. Wow—absolutely perfect!

Looking at each other, the mother and daughter cried in unison, "Thank you, Angelina!"

A few minutes before the bewitching hour of five o'clock, Katie gave Max a quick rub, grabbed her purse and headed out the door with Amanda right on her tail, just to make sure she made it to Em's house okay. They hopped in a taxi that took them to the Landis's three-story townhouse. The cabbie drove like he was in the Grand Prix, and both mom and daughter held on for dear life.

Katie kissed her mom goodbye at Emily's steps and rushed to the front door. Katie could hear the girls laughing and chatting in the living room as she closed the door behind her. A quick glance around the room told Katie this was definitely going to be a very magical night. All her friends were wearing different colors and styles and everybody looked so hot. It seemed like they all grew older and sophisticated just since the three o'clock school bell rang. How did that happen so fast?

Emily was stunning in a black velvet skirt that almost reached the floor. She wore an ivory satin blouse with pearls scattered in random abstract designs. Pearl and diamond earrings studded her ears, a birthday gift from her parents. Those earrings were awesome, and Em had the good sense to wear her hair up so they would really be noticed. Katie's BFF could have been on the cover of *Seventeen*!

Katie stood in the ornate arched doorway for a minute, feeling much like Alice stepping through the looking glass. She sensed she was entering a new life with her childhood left behind. Was this what growing up was all about?

When Emily and the others noticed Katie framed in the heavy oak doorway, a collective gasp filled the room. They couldn't believe the transformation! Maybe it was because Katie usually dressed in casual clothes in neutral colors, or maybe it was because she didn't usually wear make-up, or maybe it was because she actually glowed! Whatever was happening, Katie owned the room for that moment in time.

After a minute of congratulating each other on how good they looked, Emily's dad called out, "Let's go, the limo is here!"

Nine exceptionally eager girls fell all over each other getting into the stretch white limo. Just like in the movies, it was stocked with sodas and bags of snacks. A TV was placed high above the glass partition separating the girls from the driver. What else but a DVD of Justin Beiber would be playing? The baby-faced teen was crooning, *You know you love me, I know you care; Just shout whenever, and I'll be there.* Each girl hugged the edge of the leather seat, looked up at the video image and fantasized Justin was singing only to her. The girls sang along with their guy, and knew every word.

Before long, the long car took a sweeping right turn at the entrance to the stately Pelham Country Club. It seemed impossible such a place surrounded by acres of green was located twenty minutes from Manhattan. The girls stared out the window in surprise. What a fabulous welcome to the party!

The maître d' welcomed the Landis family guests with a bow and shook hands with each girl. He then led the party to a large round table covered in pale lavender linen. An enormous floral arrangement of white, pink and red roses accented with massive fern fronds stood tall and full in the center of the table.

Jessica, Em's funniest friend, proclaimed she was glad they were sitting under such a big umbrella, just in case the candles caused the sprinkler system to gush all over them.

Deep purple and pink place cards spelled each girl's name in rhinestones and glitter. Katie couldn't help but think of Angelina—she would just love all this glamour.

Two waiters, Juan and Steven, were assigned to the table, and this duo sure knew how to do things right. With a magician's flourish, they whipped a pink napkin from each table setting and laid it on the closest lap. Lemon slices were added to the iced water, and a sprig of mint was offered. A glass of water never looked so fancy!

Dinner began with a shrimp cocktail—whoa, those babies had to be on steroids! They were the size of Montana! A spinach salad topped with dried cranberries, candied walnuts, and feta cheese was served next, and then a choice of lobster tail or filet mignon was offered as the entrée. Since most of the girls had no clue how to dig for lobster meat, and if they did, didn't want to risk a fork-to-mouth malfunction, all opted for the beef. Stuffed potatoes, almondine green beans, and sautéed mushrooms filled the plates, which were garnished with sprigs and squiggles of who knows what. It was a feast extraordinaire!

After the table was cleared, a large white linen envelope was placed before each guest with a single red rose laid over it. What could the party favor be? Enthusiastically the girls ripped open the envelopes. iTunes gift cards! Every single one of them would undoubtedly be used for Justin-inspired tunes.

"Thank you, Emily," the girls cried in unison, with definite sing-song styling.

As they waited for Emily's birthday cake to make its grand entrance, Emily opened her gifts. A Coach bag started the present parade, with beaded bracelets, sweaters, iPod accessories and earrings falling close behind.

Katie's gift was the last one left to open. Giggling over the excessive use of glam, Em slowly unwrapped the silver box.

Lifting the last of the tissue paper, there laid the beautiful monogrammed bracelet she had wanted for a long time! She and Katie had seen the bracelet in a "What's Hot" magazine column months before and Emily was touched that her best friend remembered how much she liked it. How lucky Emily felt to have such a thoughtful friend, but Katie herself was the best gift ever!

With a drum roll sounding from the band playing in the far corner of the room, Juan and Steven led a conga line of smiling, singing waiters to the Landis table—their deep voices making Em's Happy Birthday song sound like a rousing show tune. They gathered around Emily and serenaded her three times before each giving her a big brotherly hug.

Finally the maître d' wheeled in the cake.

It was a work of art! The chocolate iced cake was four tiers tall and was created in a jagged pyramid that looked like stacked CDs and DVDs, with Justin's image plastered on every sugared label. Knowing Emily loved raspberry, caramel, lemon, and fudge fillings, and always had a hard time making up her mind which to choose, her mom made sure each tier had a generous sample of each.

Vanilla bean ice cream was mounded high on each piece of cake as it was served, and for the first time that night, silence filled the air. Everybody was too busy enjoying dessert to say much of anything.

Two pieces of cake were cut for each girl to take home and were carefully placed in white embossed boxes, then tied with a white satin ribbon. This was just like a wedding!

It took a few minutes to pack up the gifts, a job left to Em's mom and dad while the girls marched to the ladies' room. It was almost time to pile into the limo for the big event of the night. Powder room chattering soon rose to a dull roar as the girls elbowed for mirror position. This was so cool—what a night it had been so far!

Their limo driver quickly jumped from his position leaning against the car to open the doors when he spied the girls racing toward him. He was used to crazy fans, but these girls were *really* excited! He'd heard they were sitting in the front row and JB himself had granted a backstage audience. If that was true, a little craziness was definitely to be expected.

Emily was the last one in and presented the driver with a box of birthday cake to enjoy while they were at the concert. Hey, he thought, this was one nice kid!

The streets were almost impassable the closer they got to the theater where JB was the happening event. Tickets had been sold out for weeks, but that didn't stop thousands of wild fans from lining the streets hoping for a glimpse of their idol.

As the Landis long white party limo slowly crept along, fans thought maybe *this* was the one carrying Justin. Emily and her entourage were excited, but still a tiny bit frightened, as screaming, crying girls rushed the car. Katie leaned back in her seat and thought, so this is what it was like to be a star. Maybe it wasn't so much fun after all. It seemed a lot of privacy had to be sacrificed for fame and fortune.

The driver maneuvered the limo to the front doors where stern-faced guards checked the girls' names against a master list as each left the car. Concert-goers in the first ten rows were subject to security clearance, just as a precaution. Even this extra attention added to the rush the girls were feeling.

Following an usher who couldn't possibly be heard above the roar of the crowd, the girls found their way to the front row with the help of a pulsating flashlight. The closer they got to their seats, nasty comments were hurled their way—"Too good to sit back here with us? Hey, who do you think you are? Wiggle it, babies, but not at us!"

Sheesh, Em worried, I hope my friends aren't scared!

Anticipation reached fever pitch when the stage lights suddenly dimmed. A burst of fireworks exploded behind the backdrop and the audience fell quiet, but just for a moment. Then a collective sigh of disappointment echoed. Before Justin would start his grind, two warm-up bands were scheduled to take the stage. They were good, very good, but nothing like the real thing.

As the curtain fell on The Wild Ride Rockers, the auditorium plunged into total darkness. A hush fell over the hundreds filling the seats. This had to be what they were waiting to see! A rainbow of lights violently arched across the stage, synchronized to the beat of *Baby.* Fog machines created an eerie vapor causing the moving colors to whirl wildly. Launching from deep beneath the platform, JB rose to his rock throne surrounded by masses of screaming, crying girls.

What was going through his mind right now, Katie wondered. Did he even see faces in the throng of adoring teens?

Dressed in black leather from head to toe, JB was prime! With back-up dancers mimicking every move, Justin loomed bigger than life. He sang every top single on the charts— *Somebody to Love, Favorite Girl, Never Let You Go, Down to Earth*—and had every girl in the audience thinking he was singing only to her. What a gift of talent that guy owned!

After the intermission, Justin came back on stage and interacted with his fans in a more casual way. He chatted and strutted with the mic in hand and reached out . . . to the front row! As his hand grasped those of Emily's guests, they were so awed they couldn't respond to his touch—something they would kick themselves about later. The girls were transfixed, not able to join the screeching going on around them. This was their dream come true.

Emily's parents sat in the second row and took it all in. They poked each other as they remembered the Duran Duran and Madonna concerts when they acted exactly the same way. Some things just never change.

After the final encore, a crazy mixed up version of *Stuck in the Moment* and *Latin Girl*, Emily and her friends pulled out their make-up to get ready for the backstage meet. No way could they get to the rest room for the final primp, the crowd still crammed the aisles. The stage manager would sneak them through a side door.

As Katie reached into the little lavender purse Angelina had given her, she felt a lump in the lining. Wiggling the satin lining from side to side, she worked the bumpy object free. There in her hand was an incredible golden ring with a large, very large, deep green stone surrounded by diamonds. Wow!

Katie quickly placed the ring deep in her purse. She would get a better look once she got home, now certainly wasn't the time.

Before they knew it, Em and her entourage were face to face with Justin. He looked like he'd just run a marathon and was chugging a can of soda. Offering the girls a can, he asked them to sit down so they could talk. He wanted to know which songs they liked best, and then asked about their lives. This couldn't be happening!

His manager appeared with a stack of photos and Justin took the time to sign each with a personal note. On Katie's he wrote, *To Katie, the beautiful blond girl who's wearing purple and pink, my favorite colors!*

After the girls' fifteen minutes of fame, Justin rose to leave. Before he left, he reached to Emily and held her in his arms. He gave her a birthday kiss, and Katie thought her BFF was going to faint.

With a wink and a flash of his famous grin, he was off. No one moved for at least a minute and then the girls exploded into a human scream machine that went on for at least three minutes. This was so much better than they ever dreamed it would be. What could Emily possibly do as an encore for her next birthday?

Like Cinderella's coach, the long white limo was waiting to break the night's spell. *Home by midnight . . . home by midnight . . . home by midnight . . .* then on to relive it all in dreamland.

Amanda was eagerly waiting for Katie, Max was too. How in the cat's world did he know Katie would have a box of cake with her?

"Mom, you won't believe what a night I had!"

"The limo, the club, the dinner, the cake, the waiters, the concert, and Justin too! I'm definitely in love. He winked at me, Mom, he actually winked at me! OMG, I'm going to faint. And, look—he signed a picture just to me! I'm going to hang this right by my bed so I can dream of Justin every night."

Katie babbled on and on. Being young once herself, Amanda knew the feeling. "I'm so happy you had a fun time, now go get in your pjs. It's so late. You looked so good. I'm really glad we bought the outfit, and the way you wear that purse across your front is really cool."

The purse! Katie suddenly remembered the ring.

"Mom, look what I found in the purse." Katie pulled the emerald ring from the bottom of the lavender bag and showed Amanda.

"What in the world? You found it in this bag, where?"

"It was buried in the lining; look there's a little hole deep on the right side. It must have gotten stuck in it, or else somebody was trying to hide it."

"Wow, it looks like an emerald and they sure look like diamonds." exclaimed Amanda. "Let me put it in a safe place. In the morning we'll go to Hansen's Jewelry Store and see if it's real. It might be just a copy."

"Mom, if it *is* real, it could be worth a lot of money and its mine because I found it!" Katie was so excited she could hardly catch her breath.

"Katie, whoa girl, hold on just a minute. The purse belonged to someone before we bought it, and the ring was in the purse when that person brought it to *Miracles* to consign for charity. We need to think about this first and try to find the owner. Don't you think that would be the right way to handle this?"

Amanda was fighting the thought that this ring could be worth a small fortune and if they did sell it, who would know? Well, she thought. *I* would know, and I would also know it was the wrong thing to teach my daughter.

"Katie, let's go to visit Angelina tomorrow morning to find out who consigned the outfit. On the way we'll stop at Hansen's and see what he says before we get all excited over nothing. But if it is real, Angelina can tell us whose little purse this was. I have to make the final payment on your outfit anyway. The shop was closed when I stopped by the other day. Let's have lunch while we're downtown too, just to celebrate each other."

Lunch sounded fun, but Katie's heart sank all the same. "Give it back? Mom, please, no!"

But Katie knew she would never win this argument. In her heart she knew her mom was right. If she had been the one who lost the ring, she would want it returned.

Now she hoped the ring wasn't real, and then giving it back would be easy.

"Good night, Mom," Katie yawned as she headed to her room. The concert was over and it was absolutely fabulous, but now she had to figure out what to do about this ring.

She was so tired she couldn't keep her eyes open another minute. Well, maybe just a few seconds to look at Justin's picture again.

CHAPTER FOUR

As Green As Could Be

After a quick breakfast of toast and jam the next morning, Amanda and Katie headed downtown.

It was a beautiful sunny day, but Katie felt a dark cloud looming when she thought about giving up the emerald ring. Even if it was a fake, it was pretty and looked so awesome on her finger.

Entering the old jewelry store, Amanda introduced herself and Katie to Woody Hansen, the store's 80-year-old owner. She explained they wanted to know if a piece of jewelry was genuine.

Mr. Hansen reached in his big oak desk for his well-used loupe and adjusted the small magnifier to his eye. He examined the ring for a full five minutes.

"Not only is this ring real, Madame, it is perfect in color and has no visible flaws. This is quite a fine piece of jewelry! In my expert opinion, but please keep in mind I haven't done a detailed examination, I am fairly sure it would be worth around one hundred thousand dollars, possibly more. Are you intending to sell it?"

Katie and Amanda stared at each other. Amanda could tell what was going through her young daughter's mind. Katie was no doubt thinking this was a real miracle knocking on their door, and Amanda was forcing herself from thinking that same thought.

"No, sir, we're not planning to sell the ring. Thank you for your time and honesty," Amanda finally answered, knowing the ring was not theirs to sell.

"Mom! Can you believe what Mr. Hansen just told us!" Katie could hardly talk coherently as they hurriedly left the store.

"Yes, I do believe it, Katie, Mr. Hansen is an expert on gems." Amanda was fighting to regain her composure after hearing the stunning news.

As the mother and daughter continued down the street to *Miracles Can Happen,* Amanda held her purse carrying the ring close to her, even closer than before.

A bell tinkled merrily as they opened the door to *Miracles* and there stood Angelina to welcome them, angelic as always. Opening her purse and counting dollar bills one by one, Amanda made the final payment on the dress.

Never say never, Amanda thought to herself, pleased that things had worked out so well.

"So tell me dear Katie, how was the party?" Angelina asked pleasantly.

"Just great, just so, so great," Katie replied enthusiastically "Thank you so much for helping us. I had a super time."

Amanda started explaining about the found ring, before she could change her mind.

"Angelina, we need to get in touch with the person who brought in the outfit and little purse. We have a very important matter to discuss with them."

Angelina glanced at the pair, a knowing look creeping over her face.

Amanda continued rapidly, "We found something we believe the owner might have left in the purse by mistake. We must *only* speak with her about this matter," Amanda added adamantly.

"Well, that certainly sounds quite important. Let me check my records." Angelina disappeared behind a curtain of gauzy clouds that hid her tiny office.

When she reappeared a few minutes later, she had the name and address of the owner in her hand.

"Here it is. The outfit, ballet flats and evening bag belonged to a Miss Ashley Cummings." Angelina carefully folded the pink parchment paper in half and handed it to Amanda.

Amanda and Katie thanked the little old lady and once again left *Miracles Can Happen*, knowing what they had to do when they got home. But first, a fancy lunch was in order. Amanda hoped this would make Katie feel a little bit better.

Unable to contain her excitement as the door closed behind the mother and daughter, Angelina stretched her arms to the star-studded ceiling and pirouetted around the room. This was her elegant, but elderly version of a happy dance! A smile crossed Angelina's crinkled rosy cheeks as she eagerly anticipated what was to come.

A few blocks away, Katie and her mom enjoyed tiny sandwiches and delicate sweets at Tassie's Tea House, the fanciest place they could find for their celebration lunch. With glasses of pink lemonade, they toasted their decision to make Miss Ashley Cummings one very happy girl. Katie tried not to choke on her words!

Once back in the apartment, Katie snuggled deep in her favorite chair and started writing her letter to Ashley. Finding no special stationery to use for this important letter, Katie decided a plain piece of paper would just have to do.

Careful not to describe what she had found hidden in the purse, Katie kept her letter very short. She simply wrote she found something that might possibly belong to the original owner of the outfit she had purchased at a charity consignment shop. She left it up to Ashley to name what it was. Katie would not give her one hint. Not even that it was green!

Katie finished the letter, walked to the post office and dropped it in the slot. As she heard the letter drop, she closed her eyes and wished Miss Ashley Cummings would never send an answer!

CHAPTER FIVE

Oh, No!

Every day Katie rushed home from school to check the mail. Katie had expected an immediate response to her letter, and was surprised when weeks turned into months and there was still no word from the mysterious Miss Ashley Cummings.

Katie was beginning to think, and hope, the ring would be hers after all!

Katie told Emily all about the ring and the two spent hours speculating about its owner. They made up all kinds of stories, including one where the ring was hidden by an Iranian double agent and smuggled out of her country in the heart-shaped purse, then ditched in a ravine when she was found out.

After two long months passed, Amanda told her anxious daughter that if she had heard nothing by the end of the next month, she could keep the ring.

Yes! This was just what Katie wanted to hear!

The Cummings family had just returned from a two-month trip to Europe. Fortunately the private school Ashley attended understood the lifestyle Ashley and her dad Peter shared. Often, a private tutor traveled with them to make sure Ashley's grades were maintained. Along with the Cummings' housekeeper Bertie, Tutor Thompson had accompanied Peter and Ashley on their extended trip. Robert, the in-house Cummings' handyman, driver and all-around jack-of-all-trades, stayed home to care for the palatial mansion.

Today, their first full day home, Peter and his young daughter waded through the stacks of mail piled high on the entryway table. When Peter left to answer the phone, Ashley continued to plow through the fourth tall stack of envelopes.

In the middle of the mound was a plain white envelope addressed to Ashley. She couldn't imagine who was using the post office since texting was her communication of choice. She had to read the carefully written message twice to make sure she wasn't dreaming!

"Bertie, Bertie, come quickly!"

Bertie ran down the back steps so fast that she had trouble catching her breath. When she saw Ashley so animated and excited, she worried something awful had happened.

"What's going on?" The elderly housekeeper wheezed as her words struggled to be heard.

Ashley rushed to say, "You'll *never* believe this, Bertie, somebody found my ring!"

"Oh, my Lord," exclaimed Bertie. "This surely must be a special person to want to give it back."

"Read the letter, Bertie. I have to write back *now*! Oh, Bertie, let me get you a glass of water first. I didn't mean to scare you."

Scanning the one page letter as Ashley poured a glass of water, Bertie felt a chill. This was some kind of miracle, she was sure of it.

Ashley frantically searched the top desk drawer for the sweetly scented stationery with the big letter *A* curlicue at the top. Sweet delicate spring flowers bordered the pale lavender parchment paper. It had been designed just for Ashley at a store in London.

As she began to write, Ashley realized the letter had been sitting unanswered for so long that this Katie Richards must be wondering why she never heard anything back. She hoped Katie hadn't given up on her!

Slowing down, Ashley thought for awhile before she started writing; she wanted her response to be perfect and to show how grateful she was for Katie's kindness. Describing the ring in great detail so there was no mistake, she closed by asking Katie to call her when she received her letter. Glancing at the clock, Ashley realized the last mail pick-up at the post office would be in fifteen minutes! She begged Bertie to take the letter to Robert so he could make it to the box in time.

Bertie ran down the steps, letter in hand and called Robert to the house.

"Robert, Miss Ashley has a special request for you."

With a precise English accent Robert responded politely, "And what would that be, Bertie?"

"Someone found Ashley's emerald ring that was misplaced many months ago. You know, the one we turned the house upside down to find."

"Where in the world was it?"

"That we don't know, except a girl named Katie who lives in the city has it. Ashley wrote Katie to confirm it's the same ring and she wants to get her letter in the mail today. Hopefully the girl will call so we can find out what happened."

"Don't say another word, off I go. Just tell Mr. Cummings I had to run an errand. Ashley can explain the rest."

"Never a dull moment!" exclaimed Bertie as she headed back to the house. It was time to start dinner. It felt good to be home and in her own kitchen again. Eating out was fun when they traveled, but she couldn't wait to fix her favorite old recipes again. There's no place like home, Bertie sighed.

Robert barreled down the driveway and made it to the post office just as the clerk was emptying the big brass box. The letter was now on its way to Katie Richards, and who knew what would happen next.

Several days later Katie bounced down the steps to the box where the mailman left their mail every day. It had been cold and snowy for about a week and this was the first day she didn't have to worry about slipping on packed ice. The janitor sprinkled a double dose of salt on the steps to melt the inch of ice that had accumulated after days and days of snow. Katie took off her heavy gloves, slipped her postal key into the latch and opened the tiny box.

As she always did, Katie reached in and grabbed the mail, placed it in a canvas bag, and then climbed the steps back to the apartment.

Since she was short on time that particular day, Katie threw the bag on the recliner and started the laundry. Before it was time to set the table for dinner, Katie decided to sort through the day's mail.

It was near the first of the month so expected bills filled the bag. But stuck between the stack of privacy envelopes was one that caught Katie's immediate attention.

The written address commanded the entire front of the lavender linen envelope with the script scrolled and flourished, almost like calligraphy. Katie turned the envelope to see the return address. Oh, no! It read *Miss Ashley Cummings!*

"Well, Miss Cummings," murmured Katie, "what took you so long?" With a sense of dread creeping over her, Katie opened the envelope and carefully removed the letter.

> *Dear Katie,*
>
> *I am so sorry I didn't get in touch with you sooner. My father and I have been traveling in Europe and just returned home to South Hampton. I was so excited to hear from you and so happy you enjoyed wearing my outfit. I'm only praying that what you found was a ring.*

You see, my mother died and left me a very special emerald and diamond ring. The first time I wore it, I noticed it was too big for my finger. I was afraid I might lose it, so I put it in the pink bag I was carrying that night. I thought it would be safe. But, when I got home and opened the bag to get the ring, it was gone! I cried and cried for weeks over it and finally gave up searching.

Yes, Ashley, Katie said to herself as her eyes welled with tears. I found your ring.

For a split second Katie considered pretending she never got the letter. Then she could keep the ring!

No, that wouldn't happen. Her mother had always taught her the right thing to do, and lying about the letter would never be the way to go. Katie could hear her mom saying, "If you do the right thing, good things in life will come to you." Katie continued reading, hoping her mom knew what she was talking about!

I'm enclosing my phone number. It's an unlisted number and I hope you'll call when you get this letter. Maybe you could come over one Sunday so we could get to know each other.

Oh, I pray it's my mother's ring you found!

Ashley had no more words to write except . . .

Thank you, Katie, and please call.

Katie read the letter over and over again until she could recite each word without looking at the paper. This was one of the worst days of her life.

CHAPTER SIX

Could It Get Any Worse?

Amanda came home from work to find Katie waiting on the steps leading to the apartment. Behind her, the door was left wide open and gave the perfect opportunity for Max to escape to explore the neighborhood. What was Katie thinking? Amanda immediately knew something was terribly wrong, but what could have happened to upset Katie so much?

"Katie, what is it?" Amanda demanded, her voice filled with concern.

"It finally came."

For a moment Amanda had no idea what Katie was talking about.

"The letter, Mom, the letter from Ashley finally came," Katie whispered between sobs.

Amanda sat down beside Katie and tried to digest this unexpected news. She became very worried when she saw how the letter had affected her daughter.

"Let me see it, please."

Katie slowly handed Amanda the letter. She read it quickly without saying a word.

After a few minutes of silence, Amanda urged tenderly, "It sounds like this ring is very special to Ashley, regardless of the cost. Please give her a call to set her mind at ease."

"Right now, yes, I'll do it right now," Katie insisted. She wanted the whole disappointing mess put behind her, the sooner, the better!

Katie grabbed the phone with a shaking hand and dialed Ashley's number. For what seemed like an eternity the phone rang and rang, and then finally a woman's voice answered.

"Cummings' Residence," the voice stated in an authoritative, distinctive manner.

Katie stammered, "Ash . . . Ashley Cummings, please."

Katie waited and waited. Finally, a young girl's voice came across the line. "This is Ashley, who's calling, please?"

"Hi, my name is Katie Richards . . ."

Before she could say another word, the girl on the other end cried, "Katie! Thank you so much for your letter! I'm so glad you called too. Tell me, did you find a ring in the little purse?"

"Yes, Ashley, I did find a ring, and it sounds like it's *your* ring from your description," Katie sighed.

"That's wonderful news! Do you think you could come to my house in the Hamptons next weekend, maybe Sunday?" Ashley asked hopefully.

"Ashley, I don't think my mom and I can get there, we don't have a car," Katie answered. This was moving too fast!

"I'm sure my dad can arrange to have someone pick you up. Please, please say you'll come!"

Katie was confused. Shouldn't Ashley be coming to get the ring? Why should they have to make the trip, even if it was to the Hamptons?

Unsure how to handle the situation, Katie turned to her mom for an answer.

"Mom, Ashley invited us to her house next Sunday, should we go if her dad can send a car to come get us?"

"Well, I'll try to get off work, but I have the chance to work a double shift that day and we can use the money. But I'll ask if I can trade days with one of the other waitresses."

Amanda wasn't sure about this visit at all, but she did want to get this ring issue cleared up and settled. It was too upsetting for Katie to continue on this way.

"Ashley, if my mom can get off work, we'll come," Katie promised, thinking this might be a really bad idea.

"Great! If it works out, just call and my dad will have a car come for you at eleven o'clock Sunday morning. It will take about two and a half hours to get here. Is that okay?"

"Yes, that will be fine," replied Katie. She knew it was a beautiful drive and it would do them both good to get out of the city.

"Talk to you soon, Katie!"

Ashley hung up and Katie snuggled in the comfortable recliner she liked to call all hers. She gathered Max in her arms and snuggled with him to hide the tears streaming down her cheeks. She didn't want her mom to see how upset she was.

Enough of this pity party, Katie scolded herself as she ran to call Emily.

Not even bothering to say hello, Katie blurted, "It's over for me! It came, it finally came!"

"Katie, calm down a minute. What came? Oh, no, not the letter! What does it say? Read it to me."

Katie read the words so fast that Emily had to tell her to slow down. She wasn't getting one word of this.

"Can you believe this girl wants *me* to come to her and to give her the ring? How bad is that? What's she thinking?"

"Listen, Katie, she's probably some spoiled rich brat from the Hamptons and is used to getting her way. But I would get it over with once and for all, as fast as you can. You know how your mom feels. You have to give the ring back. I guess maybe you could make it an adventure. Who knows, maybe it won't be so bad. Sending a car for you too—isn't that fancy!"

Another ride in a limo, Katie thought, well, yes, that couldn't be *all* bad.

"Alright, I guess I have to go. If you weren't going to Disney this weekend, I'd make you come with me, Em."

"You can call or text me while I'm gone and tell me what happened," her BFF assured her.

With that thought, Katie said good-bye, feeling a little better but still wishing she could keep that ring. She took it out of the pouch and tried it on for the thousandth time. It sparkled so much! Oh well, forget it, this bauble was going back to its home in the Hamptons. Feeling pangs of sadness, Katie replaced the emerald ring in the velvet drawstring bag and hid it away for the last time.

The next day Katie decided to stop by *Miracles* to visit with Angelina. She often popped in the little store and was growing quite fond of Angelina. Katie especially loved the stories the little lady told about growing up in the country on the outskirts of London.

The little bell tinkled a welcome as Katie opened the door. As always, Angelina greeted her with a warm, wide smile and a gentle hug.

"So what brings you in today, my little Katie?"

"Angelina, do you know Ashley Cummings? She's the girl who consigned the outfit I bought from you."

"Not really, my dear," Angelina replied, an odd look filling her face. "Why do you ask?"

"Oh, just wondering. I was just thinking about her and something she left in the little bag by mistake. I might be going to her house to return it and I was hoping you could tell me something about her."

Katie debated telling Angelina about the expensive ring, but decided she should check with her mom first.

"Katie, the outfit was brought in by a housekeeper, or maybe it was a nanny. She had an unusual name, like a bird. Yes! Her name was Bertie!"

Oh, great, Katie thought, Ashley has a nanny no less.

Always the hostess, Angelina went to the back room and brought out a tray of cookies iced in pale yellow and highlighted with daisies delicately designed with edible paint. A crystal pitcher of lemonade was set on a small table.

No one else was in the shop, Katie noticed. It must be a quiet day.

"Katie, I have a little gift for you. It's a necklace and locket I've loved wearing for years, and I think you might enjoy it now." Reaching under the counter, Angelina presented Katie with a small clear box holding the necklace.

"Oh, no, Angelina, I couldn't possibly accept this—it looks so expensive." The gold heart-shaped locket hanging from the heavy chain was very ornate and appeared to be an antique. It was etched with heavy botanical designs and almost looked like a frenzied floral fantasy.

"Oh, but you must accept it, Katie! I want you to remember me always. Your visits mean so much to this little old lady. Please enjoy wearing the locket as much as I have."

Angelina gently fastened the locket around Katie's neck. "Keep it close to you, my dear, and perhaps your dreams will come true one day; mine certainly have."

After a long visit, Katie left the shop feeling better about everything. Angelina had a wonderful way about her and possessed the gift of bringing a sense of peace to everyone she met.

Feeling lighthearted, Katie skipped home. Max was waiting regally by the door ready for a good scratch, if not a snack. Standing at the hall mirror, Katie examined the beautiful heart around her neck.

Hey, the locket had the letter *K* swirled among the flowers and leaves. It should have been an *A* for Angelina. Then Katie realized Angelina must have had the *K* inscribed when she decided to gift the jewelry to her. She was so thoughtful! Katie would treasure this little heart forever.

After her conversation with Katie, Ashley went into the study where her father was holding a meeting. It seemed he spent a lot of time discussing business these days, but still he always made time for her.

"Daddy, may I speak to you for a moment?"

Tears were brimming in Ashley's eyes and when her dad saw that, nothing mattered except what his daughter had to tell him.

Since the death of his wife Anne two years before, Peter Cummings devoted himself not only to his work, but also to his daughter. He wanted Ashley to have all the love and attention her mother had showered on her when she was alive. It was not easy with his crazy schedule and heavy social demands, but Peter vowed he would work hard to make his young daughter as happy as she could be.

"Ashley, what is it, darling? What's wrong?"

Ashley answered with a sob, unable to talk about how happy Katie had just made her feel.

Turning to the men gathered in the study, Peter announced, "Guys, let's take a ten minute break."

"Oh, Daddy, Katie called and she does have mom's ring! Can you believe someone actually found it and is returning it to us?" Ashley was genuinely amazed.

Peter never thought they would see the ring again. He was sure if it were ever found, the lucky soul would surely chant, "Finders keepers, losers weepers" and sell the keepsake that had been so important to his family.

Peter had not been able to scold Ashley at the time of the loss. The loss of her mother was devastating enough. He assured her accidents happened all the time and her mother wouldn't want her to cry over an old ring. Now he couldn't believe someone was actually offering to return the piece of antique jewelry.

Anne had loved antiques, and even when Ashley was a baby, would take her to store after store searching for old treasures. As she grew, Ashley learned to love old things as much as her mother did.

The Monday Anne and her young daughter discovered the emerald ring during one of their jaunts was really a special day. They were told by the antique shop owner that the ring was supposedly once owned by a princess who felt it brought her good luck whenever she wore it. At the time both Anne and Ashley wondered why the princess would ever give up such a ring, but were glad she did. It was an expensive purchase, but Anne loved wearing it and assured Ashley it would be hers one day, luck and all.

"Dad, I invited Katie and her mom over to our house this weekend, is that okay? I didn't think you'd mind."

"That's great, Ashley. I don't object at all. In fact, you absolutely did the right thing." Peter leaned down and kissed his daughter gently on the forehead.

Ashley looked up at him adoringly. She loved him so much!

"Of course Katie's welcome here anytime. She sounds like a fine young lady. She must have been brought up well to know what to do when you find something that isn't yours. Remember that, Ashley; it's a good lesson for all of us to keep close."

Peter Cummings walked back into his study to continue the meeting with his producers. Peter was the number one draw at the box office these days, and had been for many years. His movies were hits right from the start and every studio in Hollywood was after him to star in their films.

Even with all the trimmings of a movie star, Peter was a real down-to-earth guy. He was outrageously handsome and every woman he met was captured by his charm. But after the death of his wife, Peter preferred to stay at home with Ashley. He had loved his wife so very much and still couldn't bring himself to think about other women.

Peter was a wonderful father to Ashley and they doted on each other, something that surprised many. Ashley accompanied her dad on location whenever possible and they enjoyed each other's company, each seeing bits of Anne in the other.

Bertie took care of them both like a mother hen, and had been with the Cummings family for years. She helped care for Ashley from the time she was born and loved her with the warmth of a grandmother.

Bertie was the best cook and was proud to present healthy farm-to-table food for their evening meals. Ashley loved watching cooking shows with her, and often watched Reed Alexander from *Icarly* turn out "kewl" recipes on the *Today Show*. Being culinary-inspired, Ashley and Bertie would rush to the kitchen after the shows and concoct what they laughingly called "Bertie's Bodacious Bundle of the Day."

Never marrying and having to work from an early age, Bertie felt lucky to have found such a wonderful home. It was more than a place to work. She adored each and every one of them and was devastated when Anne died. All the Cummings took to Bertie's warmth immediately and it was a perfect match from the beginning. She was genuinely one of the family.

Bertie was thrilled the emerald ring was coming home after all this time. Discovering it in the antique store had been such a bonding experience for Anne and her young daughter. Many nights she heard Ashley cry herself to sleep because she had lost this dear remembrance of her mother.

Bertie smiled as she thought, no more tears. Hallelujah! No more tears would fall . . . at least over the ring.

CHAPTER SEVEN

Off We Go

Amanda was able to get Sunday off after all. Katie called Ashley a few days before to make arrangements for their trip to South Hampton. She still wasn't sure about this little jaunt, but decided it was best to get the ring out of her life if she really had to.

Katie suggested that Amanda get her hair done to celebrate their upcoming big adventure. Amanda's hair was in real need of something. It was hanging limp with no shape or style.

Okay, Amanda thought, I got a big tip last night and I could put it toward a good haircut, I guess. It's really been a while, and I do color my hair myself. She went back and forth trying to justify a visit to the salon when she finally firmly announced, "I'll go for it!"

Amanda didn't have to clock in at Cozy Corner until noon that Saturday so she made an early appointment at The Hair Affair. Once settled in her leather spa chair and soothed by Indian-inspired chants, Amanda relaxed for the first time in months.

Such pampering didn't usually happen and Amanda realized how long it had been since she took care of herself. Then her thoughts drifted to Katie.

I'm so proud of her, Amanda thought. It can't be easy for a girl of twelve to carry so much responsibility.

Amanda couldn't help but wonder about the life they would have enjoyed if they had kept the ring and sold it. Deep down she knew life could take twists and turns when least expected, and secretly worried if they did keep the ring, maybe something bad would happen as a wake-up call. They certainly couldn't afford that! She was glad they made the decision they did, but boy, what a temptation it had been.

When the shampoo assistant finished with her magic fingers, Amanda was led to the stylist's station. She texted Katie to make sure everything was okay on the home front and received her answer almost immediately: All is fine! Have fun!

Her stylist Raul was kind of cool looking, although a bit on the young side. His hair was slicked back and three earrings marched up his left earlobe. Amanda hoped he knew how to do hair for women who were thirty-something.

"What can I do for you today, Madame?" Running his fingers through her hair, Raul appeared to be analyzing its texture. He pulled and twisted as he tried to figure out what style Amanda's hair could hold.

"You're the expert, just do your thing. I only ask that it's easy to manage since I don't have a lot of time to fuss with it," Amanda's instructed.

She sat back deep in the chair and closed her eyes as Raul snipped away. Thirty minutes later she turned around to face the mirror. Surprised, Amanda swung her hair from side to side and almost didn't recognize herself. Her usual one-length, shoulder-teasing bob had been layered and feathered in a Jennifer Aniston style. She loved it! But was happy to see it could still be gathered in a ponytail when things got crazy at work.

Mentally counting the money in her pocket, Amanda decided to splurge on a make-up session. It had been years since she wore anything but True Love Pink on her lips and Misty Night on her lids.

Four young students interning at the salon made her an offer she couldn't refuse. Spend twenty-five bucks on product and they would throw in a full make-over. Without hesitating, Amanda nodded her answer—*Yes!*

Amanda figured she could use a total redo to go with her new hair style. Three girls and one guy studied her face as though they were taking her under the knife. They couldn't get over her flawless skin, especially at her age. Talk about a left-handed compliment! Amanda was amused at their serious looks as they dissected her appearance.

After much discussion, the beauty school interns picked an ivory base and a pale pink blush for starters. Amanda warned them she didn't want a heavy look and would refuse to pay if that's what they gave her. With reassuring words, they promised to keep her face as natural as could be. No theatrics!

A shimmering light gold was brushed over her lips, bringing out the flecks in her eyes. Just a touch of forest green liner highlighted her lids, but lash-lengthening mascara was applied with wild abandon.

Looking in the mirror, Amanda was surprised at how different she looked and was amazed at the transformation. Wow, she thought, this is a brand new me.

All during the procedure, salon clients gathered around Amanda's chair to watch.

"Is she a model?"

"I think I saw her on a billboard."

"Is she somebody famous trying not to be recognized?"

Amanda laughed at the whispered comments. Are they really talking about me?

When Amanda punched the time clock at work, she was bombarded with questions about her new look as compliments flowed in her direction. She must have murmured thank you a hundred times.

Katie was in the shower when Amanda arrived home from work later that night and called, "How's the haircut, Mom?"

"Oh it's shorter," Amanda teased. "You can see for yourself."

Cuddled in a white fluffy robe, Katie walked into the living room and almost screamed, thinking there was a stranger in the house!

"Wow, Mom, you look so cool. You're so, so pretty!"

"Thanks for encouraging me, Katie. Do you really like it?"
"Mom, I love it. You look outrageous!"

———⊰⊱———

Sunday morning came with the bright sun winking through the bedroom windows. Katie was actually awake long before dawn. Sleep was almost impossible on the night before she had to give up what could have been a life-changing opportunity for her and her mother. She was still feeling sorry, sad, and a little angry about giving up the lost emerald. Katie had come to think of the ring as hers, and really didn't want to part with it.

Amanda couldn't sleep much either and got up early to start the coffee. The aroma filled the small apartment and seemed to shout "Good morning, Sunshine," but was it really a good morning for them?

Today was the day they were venturing far out of the city. Amanda and Katie rarely left New York and certainly had never been to the Hamptons before. That was where the rich and famous lived!

Despite the reason for the trip, Katie was getting excited about the day's adventure. She was hoping to see a movie star or two. Katie knew most stars came to the Hamptons in the summer months, not when there was still ice and snow on the ground. But, you never know!

The car sent by Mr. Cummings was expected at eleven and as Katie and Amanda walked down the steps to wait for it, Katie suddenly cried, "Yikes, Mom! We almost forgot the most important thing!"

She ran up the stairs, rushed into the living room and reached into the drawer to search for the lavender bag that had been home to the emerald ring for so long.

After looking at the ring one last time, Katie joined her mother to wait for the car to take them to whatever the future might bring.

CHAPTER EIGHT

Unbelievable

At exactly eleven o'clock, a white limousine almost the length of the entire block pulled to a stop at the front of the Richards' apartment building. Several neighbors stopped to stare as the uniformed driver got out and opened the door for the pretty mother and daughter.

Katie and Amanda tried to appear nonchalant as if this was an everyday occurrence, but inside, both were freaking out. The driver introduced himself with a slight bow.

"Good morning, ladies. My name is Robert and I shall be taking you to the Hamptons. I assume you are Katie and Mom. Am I correct?"

"Yes sir," answered Katie without waiting for her mother to speak. A limo driver with a British accent—this was awesome! Em was right. This was going to be an adventure, at least for the day.

Making sure the ladies were comfortable with their seat belts fastened, Robert began his round of instruction. He politely showed them where the drinks and snacks were located, and how the CD and DVD players worked. He handed them the remote control for the television sitting high on a small shelf in the corner of the car.

"There are plenty of DVDs to watch. Please sit back, relax, and enjoy the ride."

Katie took out her cell and quickly texted Emily: In limo—will check in later. OMG.

Robert raised the glass partition to give privacy to his passengers and soon the long car merged into the heavy city traffic.

Katie looked at her mom and started giggling. Amanda was grinning like a Cheshire cat—a grin so wide that her cheeks started to hurt. This absolute luxury would be theirs to enjoy for the next two hours!

Katie loaded one of the DVDs she guessed Ashley had placed in the car for her. Harry Potter blasted on the screen shrieking madly as he flew through the night sky.

Amanda slid back in her seat and closed her eyes. She wanted to catch a nap so she could enjoy the day ahead. She was exhausted from working double shifts all week so she could take Sunday off.

Katie glanced at the movie, but mostly stared out the window at the moving scenery. They traveled on the Long Island Expressway passing the townships of Glen Cove, Huntington Station, Brentwood, and Riverhead. This world was so different from the one they'd left behind.

Katie didn't close her eyes for one second. She didn't want to miss a thing. The trees were still bare, but today they looked beautiful. After two hours of driving, Robert took a turn to the right leading to a small country road. Large tree limbs created an arch across the road and Katie could only imagine how pretty it must be in the spring when the trees would be full and very green. It would be a canopy!

As planned, Robert called the house to let Ashley know they would be arriving soon. She wanted a heads up about what this Katie was like.

"Ashley, I must say, both mother and daughter are very nice."

"Thanks for the late-breaking update," Ashley teased. "I'll be waiting at the front door. Give a honk and Bertie and I will come out to meet you."

"Okay," Robert answered, thinking this was going to be a very good day indeed.

After a winding mile of evergreen topiaries and skeleton-like winter gardens, Robert finally guided the white limo onto driveway paved in red brick. He slowed when he reached what appeared to be some type of entrance, although a house wasn't visible anywhere.

Robert tapped a switch and Amanda and Katie watched the pair of iron gates separate majestically. This was unbelievable!

They traveled down the drive for a few minutes when suddenly an enormous house appeared in front of them.

Katie nudged Amanda to wake her, and then knocked on the glass to get Robert's attention.

He quickly lowered the partition.

"Mr. Robert," Katie started, trying to sound very cool. "Is this Ashley's house?"

"Yes, young lady, it certainly is," Robert replied. He had been glancing in the rear view mirror to watch his passengers' reaction to what stood before them.

He had been awed the first time he saw the mansion. It was one of the biggest houses he had even seen, even in London. The house was three stories, and looked as wide as a football field.

Katie gasped when she saw the large stone fountain centered in the entrance loop. "Yikes, this is amazing," she whispered to her mom.

Amanda whispered back, "Here we go, Katie!"

As soon as he parked the car, Robert jumped out and opened the rear door for the beautiful mother and her delightful daughter.

Out of the corner of her eye, Katie saw one of the huge front doors swing open. Her first thought was how much muscle it must take to open one of those babies!

Out came Miss Ashley Cummings, or so Katie assumed. She was surprised to see Ashley seated in a wheelchair. She seemed very comfortable in it, and easily maneuvered down the shallow steps. With her smile beaming as bright as sunshine, Katie could tell Ashley was very happy to see them. She walked over to meet her hostess and offered her hand, but Ashley opened both arms for a hug.

Dressed in jeans and a white tee, Ashley Cummings was not at all what Katie expected. Her hair was a rich auburn and her eyes were deep dark green. She's so pretty, Katie thought.

"Hi, I'm Ashley. It's so great you both could come today!"

"Thanks for inviting us," Amanda answered warmly.

"Please come in." Leading the way, Ashley wheeled up the side ramp and swished through the heavy doors leading to a black and white marble foyer. In the center, a dark wooden circular table held an Oriental vase filled with draping tulips of every color imaginable.

Overhead an ornate crystal chandelier sparkled as rays from the sun pierced its intricately patterned pendants.

Off the foyer to the right was the entrance to a library where hard-cover books filled the shelves from floor to ceiling on every wall. A sliding wooden ladder was positioned to reach the ones way up high.

"Wow, you must read a lot," Katie exclaimed. Ashley and Amanda laughed at Katie's comment. Those books were meant as décor!

Looking around, Amanda said, "Ashley, what a lovely and welcoming home you have. We appreciate your kind invitation."

"I'm so happy you could come. I haven't had much company," Ashley answered sadly.

Along one wall Amanda noticed plaques awarded to Peter Cummings for acting. And then she saw the golden statues.

Suddenly it hit Amanda. Those were Oscars on the shelves! She realized she was standing in the home of the famous movie star Peter Cummings. She had seen all his movies and read every article about him she could find in magazines.

Now I'm here in his actual house! I better get ready to meet a real snob, Amanda thought. I just hope he's nice to Katie.

It was then Peter Cummings entered the library.

Extending his hand, he welcomed them saying, "How are you, Mrs. Richards? And you must be Katie. Welcome to our home. I'm Peter, Ashley's dad."

He acted just like a normal person!

Amanda had to steady herself on the back of a chair so she wouldn't faint dead away right then and there!

"Please call me Amanda. We're delighted to be here." She almost choked on her words as she struggled to act casual.

She was face to face with the most gorgeous man she had ever laid eyes on. He was more handsome in person than he was on a twenty-foot screen. His dark green eyes carried a hint of amusement as black tousled hair tumbled over his forehead and down his neck. He looked just like a movie star! Then Amanda realized, that's exactly what he was!

Looking into Amanda's eyes, Peter Cummings felt his own knees go weak. He read kindness in her blue eyes and that pleased him. Amanda and her pretty daughter would be good for Ashley he thought as he murmured, "It's a pleasure to meet you both."

CHAPTER NINE

Home, Sweet Home

Peter Cummings had known his share of beautiful women and starred with many of them over the years, but Amanda Richards was exceptional. He could sense Amanda was a woman who had not enjoyed an easy life. He knew where she and Katie lived and realized money must be a very big problem for them.

Chatting incessantly, Ashley couldn't wait to show Katie her room, but it was located on the third floor of the sprawling mansion. Katie wondered how Ashley managed to climb the steps, but then saw lifts and ramps had been installed at every staircase to make getting around easy for her.

Ashley wheeled rapidly through a maze of hallways on the way to the elevator located closest to her room and Katie could hardly keep up with her. The elevator stood ready near the kitchen to take passengers to the third floor of the house. This was going to be no problem at all.

The mansion's housekeeper was introduced as Bertie, and Katie learned it had been Bertie who came to Angelina's little store with Ashley's clothes. Bertie appeared in a doorway as the girls flew by and asked Ashley if she needed any help, but she shook her head and replied, "No, thanks."

Ashley went on to explain that Bertie had lived with them for many years, and lifted her in and out of her wheelchair every day, as well as helped her dress and bathe. In a whisper Ashley confided, "She babies me too much!"

As the girls neared Ashley's room, Katie fingered the tiny evening bag holding the precious ring. She had tucked it in the deep pocket of her blazer. Katie knew she would have to give the emerald to its rightful owner soon and tried to figure out the best way to do it.

Done in shades of pink and apple green, Ashley's bedroom was actually a four-room suite, if you counted the walk-in closet big enough to accommodate a chaise lounge. The clothes racks were motorized just like at the dry cleaners! This was really too, too much!

The main bedroom held an antique four-poster bed with mounds of lacy white pillows piled high on a down-filled flowered silk comforter. The bed was so tall that Bertie would surely have trouble lifting Ashley into it as she got older and heavier. Katie almost giggled as she thought of the fable about the princess and the pea.

A dressing table was specially built to accommodate Ashley's wheelchair, and mirrors surrounding it reflected light streaming from crystal chandeliers raining from a ceiling which had been painted with fluffy clouds. Katie was reminded of Angelina's boutique and wished her dear little friend could see all this fluff and stuff. Angelina would absolutely love it!

A smaller room to the right looked to be a media room with a computer, laptop, television, DVD player and several iPod docking stations filling the corners. The hi-tech equipment almost looked funny framed by the white walls with borders of pink azaleas teasing the ceiling and feminine organza curtains frothing at the windows. Flowering plants filled the little room, adding a cozy touch to this gleaming hi-tech world.

The most luxurious room of the four was the bath. Hand-painted botanical tiles glazed the walls over the biggest bathtub Katie had ever seen! It was a Jacuzzi with dozens of jets. A lift was suspended high on one side to help Ashley get in and out easily. The bath walls were lined with white wicker shelves loaded with pastel bath confections, bottles of colorful shampoos, and the thickest towels imaginable, all in shades of pink and green.

Connected to that room was a pretty guest room with two queen-sized beds. Katie could see it was done in white with splashes of lavender and green. Flowered pillows were scattered on the fluffy chenille bedspreads and white plantation shutters covered the windows. The afternoon sun created dancing beams on a wall, much like a painting coming alive.

Ashley invited Katie to sit in one of the chintz-covered wicker rockers so they could talk. She wheeled to a closet to get a quilt for each of them to cuddle under while they got to know each other.

Ashley was the perfect hostess Katie thought. She was beginning to feel very comfortable with this girl she hadn't expected to like at all.

Out of the blue Ashley stated matter-of-factly, "I bet you're wondering why I can't walk."

"Well, yes, I was wondering that," Katie admitted, somewhat taken back by Ashley's frankness. "But you don't have to tell me anything if you don't want to."

"But I *do* want to," Ashley said without flinching. "I was injured in a horseback riding accident several years ago. All I remember was falling off my favorite horse Blaze and waking up in the hospital unable to move my leg. My mom was helping me build my strength with physical therapy so I could walk again. Then she died and, well, that's it," Ashley said sadly as her eyes welled with tears.

"I don't know why I'm telling you all this, you probably don't want to hear it," she stammered.

"Yes, I do," Katie assured her, but was unsure of what she should say next.

A few minutes later Katie stopped rocking and asked gently, "Do the doctors think you can walk again?"

"Yes, I guess so. Please don't feel sorry for me," Ashley begged.

Changing the subject quickly, Ashley showed her guest her incredible teen treasures. Ashley wasn't bragging about her things, she was just sharing part of her life with someone she felt might be interested in what she liked.

Katie couldn't believe the posters covering the walls—they were framed even! She was shocked to see images of Justin Bieber, Selena Gomez and The Jonas Brothers signed with personal notes to Ashley. Wow—there was one from Harry Potter himself!

Ashley collected antique picture frames and little china boxes from all over the world. One shelf was filled with antique dolls Katie guessed Ashley had gotten from her mother.

Katie was full of questions about the treasures, and Ashley shared stories about the countries her family visited where she added to her collections. Each treasure had an interesting tale to tell and some were very funny.

Wow, she's been all over the place, Katie thought. Oh well, maybe one day I'll get to see someplace besides New York.

Katie suddenly felt the ring burning a hole in her pocket.

"Ashley, I have something to give you. I have your ring," Katie said hesitantly. She pulled the heart-shaped party purse from her pocket and handed it to Ashley.

Ashley smiled when she saw her old bag, and then lifted the flap to look for the ring. After clutching it to her heart for a moment, she slowly raised the emerald to the sunlight. It seemed to sparkle more than ever. Ashley placed the ring on her finger as she remembered how much it had meant to her mother.

"I don't know how to thank you, Katie. No one else in the whole world would have ever returned this ring, except you. Others would have kept it or sold it for a lot of money. I'm so lucky you were the one who bought my outfit and got that purse."

It was then that Katie realized her mom had been right all along. Pangs of guilt filled her heart when she remembered how much she wanted to keep the ring.

Her thoughts were broken when Bertie's voice roared through the intercom—"Girls, come down. Lunch is ready."

Downstairs the two parents were enjoying adult conversation. Peter was telling Amanda he never thought they would see the ring again.

"Ever since Katie called, Ashley has been a different girl. She's smiling and happy and I didn't think I would ever see her that way again. Since her mother died so unexpectedly, Ashley hasn't been the same, no matter what I do.

"When she lost the ring, I was really worried about her. Anne used to tell Ashley it was a charmed ring and would bring good luck if the emerald was rubbed in a certain way. I guess Ashley believed the story. Your kindness has been a great gift to us."

Peter gave Amanda his celebrated grin. As his words spilled out, she almost fainted.

Amanda was still awed at meeting a famous movie star, especially in his own home. Good thing I had my hair done, she joked to herself.

Together Peter and Amanda walked to the patio to join their girls for lunch. They saw the two giggling about something, just like they had known each other forever.

CHAPTER TEN

I Must Be Dreaming

Lunch was served on the expansive outdoor patio which had walls of glass so it could be enjoyed even when winter winds howled. The infinity pool had been emptied for the season, but was built in such a style that it appeared to be a multi-level sculpture without water.

The table was dressed in white with tiny pots of begonias clustered in the center. Napkins were winter white and were hotel-sized to cover much more than a lap.

Yikes, double yikes, Katie thought, this is really awesome!

Bertie created a feast for them to enjoy and placed the dishes on a casual buffet table. Along with egg salad, tuna, and turkey sandwiches, bowls of fresh fruit and pasta salads filled the table. As a special treat, Bertie baked loaves of her famous sourdough bread. The crust was so crunchy and the center so warm and soft! Who could resist taking several slices?

The conversation flowed as though both the adults and kids had known each other all their lives. Peter entertained the table with gossip about stars and Ashley added inside info about teen idols she knew. Amanda shared stories about the cast of characters filling her tables at Cozy Corner and her tales were as funny as the ones coming from Hollywood.

Once the table was cleared, bowls of ice cream made their appearance. Bertie presented two trays of toppings and placed them within easy reach. Piled high were four kinds of sprinkles, caramel, hot fudge, strawberries, kiwis, peaches, nuts, cherries, and a mound of freshly whipped cream, all ready to please the lucky lunchers.

It was easy to overload, and Katie felt if she had one more bite she would surely explode!

The four banged their spoons on the table as a call to Bertie. When she rushed out to see what the problem was, all clapped and gave her a heartfelt ovation. Although embarrassed, Bertie loved the attention.

Then Peter suggested they go into the living room for tea. Tea! Katie had never tasted the stuff and wasn't quite sure what to do if she didn't like it.

Bertie poured Earl Grey tea into bone china cups which were placed on a walnut serving cart. She explained the silver teapot had been handed down through three generations of Cummings and announced proudly that she polished it to a high gleam every single week.

Katie couldn't get over the little sugar cubes with tiny flowers and ivy iced on them. And the tea wasn't half bad. She could sure get used to this life!

Once settled, Peter began a little speech.

"Katie, Amanda, when Anne's ring was lost, needless to say Ashley and I were devastated. I placed a notice in the *New York Times* and in all our local papers."

Peter reached into a table drawer and pulled out the articles to show them.

"I offered a large reward for the ring. I am giving you the reward, which is $25,000. You certainly deserve it for being so honest. I won't take no for an answer."

Tears ran down Amanda cheeks at Peter's generosity. Katie couldn't believe what she was hearing.

Peter handed Amanda a check and gently closed her fingers around it.

"I don't know what to say, Peter!" Amanda simply stood up and walked to Peter and hugged him.

"We didn't return the ring for any other reason than it was the right thing to do."

"And the right thing to do now is for you to have the reward," replied Peter.

Now Katie was crying, along with Ashley.:

"Oh, boy, this must be a girl thing. I don't think I have enough handkerchiefs to go around," Peter chuckled.

The afternoon flew by and soon it was time to return to the city. Amanda said she had to get up early for work the next day, and Katie had school. They knew the drive back would take hours with all the Sunday traffic coming in from the Hamptons.

When Robert bought the limo around, Amanda bent down and hugged Ashley, and then squeezed Peter's hand.

Peter gave Katie an affectionate kiss on the cheek and ruffled her hair like her dad used to do when she was a little girl.

Robert, sensing the afternoon had been a success, opened the doors with a broad smile spreading over his aristocratic face. Soon the long white car started on its way.

It had been an amazing afternoon in every way. Katie made a new friend and Amanda was thinking about Peter, the first man she found interesting in a very long time.

Peter's check was tucked away in Amanda's purse and she felt relief at the sense of financial freedom it brought her and Katie. She hoped to see Peter again, but didn't think it would happen. He would probably go back to movie making and forget all about them. After all, he was a movie star and she was just a waitress.

When they arrived at the apartment, they thanked Robert and headed up the steps. There was Max sitting right inside the front door waiting to hear about their day.

But Amanda and Katie were so tired Max would have to wait. But there was no way Katie could sleep without telling Emily everything.

Tucked under her covers, she grabbed her phone and started the longest text message ever—Em, you will not believe this . . .

Katie could barely keep her eyes open, but didn't leave out one thing!

CHAPTER ELEVEN

Yes!

"Dad," Ashley began after the limo was out of sight, "I really like Katie very much. May I visit with her again?"

"I think that's a great idea! I liked Katie and Amanda too," he replied.

A few days passed, and then the week went by. Amanda was disappointed she had not heard from Peter. But why would she anyway? His world was so different from hers.

All week long Peter thought about phoning Amanda. He really wanted to get to know her better.

By the following Sunday evening Peter could wait no longer. He set any doubts aside and asked Ashley to call Katie to arrange a time for the girls to get together again.

Ashley was thrilled at her dad's suggestion and phoned Katie immediately.

Ashley planned to invite the Richards back to the Hamptons and was surprised when Katie blurted out, "Ashley, can you come to my house for dinner next Saturday? I'd love to see you again."

In the background, Amanda called, "Tell Ashley if she would like to bring her dad along, he would be most welcome. They can spend the afternoon since it's such a long trip."

She assumed Peter wouldn't be able to make it on such short notice, but still held a smidgen of hope in her heart. She was shocked when she heard Katie reply, "Great! We'll see you both next Saturday."

What was she thinking? Amanda couldn't believe she had just invited *the* Peter Cummings to their very ordinary walk-up apartment! All of a sudden she felt very insecure as her eyes traveled over the second-hand furniture filling the room. Maybe she should un-invite them? No, that wouldn't work, that would be very rude.

Oh, well, this was their home and if Peter and Ashley didn't like it, then too bad, so sad. She wouldn't pretend to be anyone other than who she was.

Now Amanda had to ask Herb for the next Saturday off. He knew about the found ring, their trip to the Hamptons, and all the amazing stuff that had happened to his favorite waitress.

The next day Herb chuckled when Amanda made her request. He couldn't help but tease her and ordered her to put her request in writing.

When he saw Amanda's face drop, he quickly reassured her, "Amanda, you're entitled to a few days off and I'm happy you're finally going to use one of them. Have fun and make sure to get an autograph for me!"

CHAPTER TWELVE

Star Light, Star Bright

The week flew by and Saturday was here before they knew it. Peter and Ashley were to arrive at two in the afternoon so they would have plenty of time together before dinner.

The Tuesday before, Amanda started searching her food files for her Eggplant Parmesan recipe, one of her favorites. It would go perfectly with her homemade tomato sauce. That recipe was handed down from her Grandma Betty's kitchen. It would take hours to prepare, but she was determined to show Peter and Ashley she could cook, and cook very well! Amanda even planned to bake homemade crusty bread to dip into the rich garlicky sauce.

Dinner would begin with a delicious salad of mixed greens and cherry tomatoes with bleu cheese sprinkled on top. Light walnut oil with a touch of seasoning would make the perfect dressing.

Dessert would be her favorite angel food cake topped with whipped cream and fresh strawberries.

Joining the excitement, Max spent his days scooting madly around the kitchen, finding no place to settle down. He knew something big was happening.

Once the menu was set, Amanda had to decide what to wear. She tried on almost everything she owned before settling on going casual. She chose a cashmere ice blue sweater and jeans that were a perfect fit.

Katie watched Amanda's impromptu fashion show and tried to understand why her mom was freaking out about what to wear. Katie, on the other hand, planned to wear her khakis from the Gap with a pale pink tee. Easy and comfy was her style.

When Saturday finally arrived, Amanda fixed her hair in the style Raul had showed her at the salon. Her hair needed a trim, but luckily still fell into place nicely. She applied her make-up, trying to remember how the students had done it. She looked in the mirror and thought, Good Lord, I'm entertaining a movie star in my home! Hang in there, Amanda, don't pass out!

Katie could hardly wait to see Ashley again. Emily couldn't believe all that had happened to her BFF over the past few weeks and loved to hear about her day in the Hamptons over and over again. Katie sensed Emily felt a little jealous so she promised could meet Ashley sometime soon. The whole adventure was taking some getting used to for everybody.

The Cummings would be arriving any minute and Katie decided to wait for them on the outside landing. When she saw the limo coming down the street she called to Amanda, "They're here!"

Amanda took several deep breaths and joined Katie to welcome their guests. Katie rushed down the steps to greet to Ashley and Peter, and of course Robert who had been so nice to them on their limo rides.

Once again neighbors peeked out their doors and windows to see what was going on at the Richards' apartment. A few gasped when they saw who got out of the car, but Peter was used to the attention and gave them a casual wave of greeting.

Peter and Robert expertly spun Ashley's wheelchair backward and bounced the chair up the stairs, with Ashley giggling wildly claiming all the jiggling tickled her funny bone. The visit was off to a wonderful start.

Catching the aromas coming from Amanda's kitchen, Peter called to Ashley, "Oh boy, somebody's cooking up a storm! I think we're in for a real treat, Ashley."

Like the gentleman Amanda thought he would be, Peter presented her with a bouquet of two dozen crimson roses tied with an ivory organza ribbon and a golden box of Godiva chocolates.

"These are for you and Katie to enjoy," Peter offered.

Peter followed Amanda into the kitchen to help place the flowers in the vase she had pulled from a cabinet. Looking for something to do, Robert began cutting the flower stems like he did for Bertie every day.

Then with a wave, Robert said he would be back for Peter and Ashley later that evening. Katie begged Robert to stay since she was growing very fond of him, but he only offered, "Next time, Katie, next time."

Robert was going to visit his nephew who lived a few miles away. He hadn't seen him in a while and they had a lot to catch up on.

"Oh, Robert," Amanda called, "I'll pack a goody box for you to take home. You and Bertie can enjoy dinner a day late. My tomato sauce is even better the next day!"

Peter walked Robert to the front door to say good-bye.

"That's some lady!" Robert whispered to his boss as he turned to leave.

"That she is," Peter agreed.

On his way back to the kitchen, Peter took in the humble surroundings. The furnishings and style were modest, and yet this home was so warm and cozy he could feel the love that filled every corner. Pictures of Katie seemed to be everywhere, many were in frames. There were photos of Amanda too, and most rested on a small table near the front window. Amanda and Katie lived a simple life, but there were so many things that made it special.

The girls were chatting about everything. Katie took Ashley into her room and showed her the program from Emily's birthday concert. They played their Bieber favorites and cranked the music up so loud it was astounding they could hear each other!

Peter found Amanda in the kitchen and started to give her a hand with dinner. The kitchen was small and they spent a good deal of time bumping into each other and laughing like kids when they did. Peter wondered if Amanda had sewed the gingham curtains hanging on the windows. He was beginning to feel there was nothing this woman couldn't do.

When the sauce was simmered to perfection, they plated the salads. Amanda had paid particular attention to the dining table which she set using her mother's Lenox china with bands of sterling silver circling the plates. Her mother's hand-cut crystal goblets and her grandmother's antique silver completed the place settings.

They called the girls and each took their assigned seat. Katie designed place cards shaped like leaves and, in her best handwriting, wrote everybody's name in a tween version of calligraphy. Flourishes and squiggles filled the cards.

In the center of the table Amanda created a centerpiece from fresh vegetables and garden herbs and placed them in an intricate wicker basket. What a fun touch for their Italian-themed dinner!

After the salad course, Peter cleared the table and went into the kitchen to help with the main course.

It was funny, he thought, he missed having family dinners where everybody pitched in to help. Bertie never let him do a thing. He found he was more relaxed than he'd been in a long time, just being with Amanda seemed to be the key.

The heirloom sauce was the best Peter had ever tasted and the eggplant was the same. Throughout dinner, conversation was lively and once again, Amanda and Katie got the inside Hollywood scoop. They loved it!

But Peter and Ashley loved hearing about Amanda and Katie's lives just as much. This was turning out to be a win-win situation!

Katie offered to clear the table, stack the dishes and get dessert. Peter jumped from his seat to help her while Amanda visited with Ashley. They chatted about the new movie her dad was starting the next week which meant traveling again. This time Ashley was staying home since she had a new tutor and Peter didn't want to disrupt her studies.

Amanda sensed Ashley was a little down about her dad being gone, but assured her Katie could visit if she'd like.

"That would be unreal! I would absolutely love, love that!"

As the grand finale, Peter and Katie dimmed the lights and carried the strawberry-heavy cake high in the air while singing *Is This All There Is?* as they paraded around the table. They were acting exceptionally goofy and Peter loved the sense of family he was feeling for the first time in years.

Amanda left the dishes for later and suggested they sit in the living room to talk. Katie brought up Peter's new movie and asked who would be starring with him.

He answered, "Julia Roberts has the lead, and I love working with her. She's a lot of fun and takes her acting seriously. She's not like some of the younger stars who stay out late and can't remember lines. Julia wants to get home as much as I do so we try to keep things moving."

Amanda settled back in her chair and thought, thank goodness she's married!

Robert returned around eleven and the evening was over too soon. The girls said their goodbyes and started counting the days until they would see each other again.

Peter and Amanda held each other's eyes, secretly hoping this would be the start of something wonderful.

CHAPTER THIRTEEN

Ashley Makes a Decision

Two weeks later plans were made for Katie to visit Ashley. Peter was flying to Los Angeles to film the first part of his new movie while Ashley stayed home as planned to study. She was comfortable with Robert and Bertie helping her, and Peter assured Amanda they would manage just fine, even with another girl in the house for the weekend.

Right before he left, Peter called Amanda to say good-bye. After a two hour conversation, he ended by whispering, "I'll miss you when I'm gone."

Amanda was surprised, but managed to respond, "I'll miss you too, and hurry back. Good luck with the movie and safe travels." Oh boy, she was falling, and falling hard!

Robert arrived as soon as school was out on Friday to take Katie to the Hamptons. With the whole back seat to herself, Katie decided to do her homework so she wouldn't have to worry about it when she got home Sunday night. That would ruin the whole weekend!

Katie borrowed a digital camera from Emily to shoot the fields of daffodils at the entrance to the Cummings estate. She knew her mom would love to see them. The bright yellow spring flower was one of Amanda's favorites. Spring came early this year and trees and flowers were budding all over the place.

Before long the big stone house loomed at the end of the drive. Ashley was waiting on the front veranda and raced her wheelchair down the walk to greet her friend.

This was going to be such a fun weekend, they thought simultaneously.

After settling in, which took about a minute, Ashley and Katie picked up where they left off a few weekends before. Bertie sent a pepperoni and mushroom pizza, a cooler filled with cola, and a plate loaded with frosted walnut brownies to Ashley's room, knowing young girls were always hungry.

Sprawled on Ashley's big bed, the two spent hours looking through old photo albums featuring the whole Cummings family. Almost every snapshot showed Ashley hanging with her mom, even when she was a baby. Anyone could see they loved each other very much. Peter was in many of the shots, but the mother and daughter team definitely stole the show.

Anne was tall and slender in the old images, with soft auburn hair framing her face just like her daughter's did now. Ashley was captured on film doing all sorts of things and appeared to be quite athletic and full of energy. Back in those days, it was probably difficult to get her to slow down long enough to make a Kodak moment materialize. Many of the snapshots also starred Blaze, the beautiful chestnut brown mare Ashley loved to ride.

With concerned interest, Katie finally asked the question that had been bugging her for some time. "Ashley, why don't you try to walk again?"

"I just don't think I can. I get around just fine in my chair and walking isn't such a big thing to me anymore," Ashley answered as her cheeks turned a soft pink.

"But, Ashley, if the doctors feel there's a good chance you *could* walk again, why do you want to spend the rest of your life living in a wheelchair? Don't you want to ride again?"

"Yes, I guess. I would love to saddle Blaze again. I miss riding so much."

Ashley had never admitted to anyone how scared she felt, but for some reason, she knew she could tell Katie anything and she wouldn't laugh or say she was ridiculous to have such feelings.

"What if I tried to walk and failed? My dad would be so disappointed and I would feel so bad."

"You'll never know if you don't try. If you *could* walk again, just think how happy and proud you would be. I know it's really scary to think about failure, but it might turn out to be wonderful for you."

Katie continued, "Ashley, why don't you let me help you? No one has to know what we're doing—it can be our secret. You can just tell me how your mother helped you, and I'll do for you what she did. Please, Ashley, say yes!"

Ashley hesitated for a moment, and then began with her round of excuses.

"Maybe you're not strong enough to hold me . . . what if you dropped me . . . maybe my legs have gotten too weak to work . . . what if I walk with a bad limp and can't do what I want to do?"

The excuses went on and on, with Katie shaking her head as each popped out of Ashley's mouth.

"Ashley, I know you can do it, but I also know I might not be strong enough to lift you. I wouldn't want to drop you ever! Let's see if Robert can help us, as least until you can build your strength a bit."

Robert came soon after Ashley called for him. He probably thought she needed help getting into a more comfortable chair so the girls could enjoy gossiping together.

When Katie told him what she had proposed to Ashley, he hesitantly agreed to help, but did have serious reservations about the whole thing.

Ashley started to sob when she thought of her probable failure and how it would affect her dad. She didn't want to build his hopes only to disappoint him. Ashley wasn't really sure if she wanted to walk again anyway; she remembered how painful the therapy had been. Even though Robert was supportive, hearing his concerns made her wonder if starting the exhaustive process all over again was worth it. After her mom died, her heart just wasn't in the effort.

"We need to settle this right now, Robert, before Ashley gives a final no," Katie urged anxiously. "I know she can do it, but it will take a lot of time and effort. The doctors would want her to try at least. Please help us, Robert!"

Still not fully convinced he should take part in this plan, Robert did agree to carry Ashley to the basement where the physical therapy machines stood like statues since Anne died two years before. He had worked with Ashley and her mother occasionally and the techniques and patterning came back to him once he saw the machines.

Digging through a desk in the basement therapy suite, Ashley found the journal her mother kept which outlined her daily exercises. She was quite surprised when she read the encouraging progress notes. At the time, she felt she was only plugging along, but maybe she was doing better than she thought she was.

Slow, heavy tears weaved down Ashley's cheeks when she finally understood how much her accident and paralysis must have devastated her mother. She'd heard mothers feel their children's pain much more than their own. At the time, she was too young to grasp what that meant.

She could and would do this! Ashley trusted Katie to help her and stay with her even when the pain tore through her body. Katie was there for the long haul, Ashley was sure of it. Robert could be talked into helping too. He wanted her dad to be happy again and Robert knew having Ashley standing on her own two feet would do it.

Ashley studied Katie's hopeful face, and then searched the doubt clouding Robert's eyes. She suddenly cried out, "Yes! We can do this!"

In an instant, Robert lifted Ashley out of her wheelchair and placed her in the swing-like contraption used to teach balance.

He massaged her legs to loosen them, and started to work the exercises he remembered doing so long ago.

Several times things just didn't go as expected. Ashley giggled uncontrollably the times Robert contorted her body like a pretzel trying to get one leg to cross the other. She was much smaller when she last used the equipment, and the trio roared when she resembled The Incredible Hulk trying to fit into the tiny harnesses. While this was serious work, it was also starting to be fun as the three kept their eye on the prize.

Katie was at Ashley's side every minute, coaxing her to try, and then try even harder. Sometimes she winced when she saw how much pain Ashley was suffering, but knew it was necessary to get her frozen muscles to respond. After an hour of effort, Ashley was too exhausted to continue, but promised she would work at it again tomorrow. She was hyped!

The basement soon became the trio's clubhouse and they christened Ashley's work-outs *Power Hours.* All weekend, Robert and Katie encouraged Ashley, wiping away her tears when things got tough and pleading with her to keep trying. Walking was not going to happen overnight, and they all knew it.

It might not happen at all, but the three warriors were committed to giving the effort their best shot.

When Sunday night rolled around and it was time for Katie to pack up, Ashley seemed down. ·

"Ashley, don't worry, I'll be back next weekend if it's okay with my mom," Katie assured her.

Holding tight to that promise, Ashley's spirits soared and a smile filled her face.

All the next week, Robert carried Ashley downstairs and worked with her whenever he had a free minute. Ashley insisted her physical therapy could only take place when Peter was out of the house. Timing was important since he would be home soon. Ashley just couldn't stand hurting her dad again if this whole effort didn't work.

When Katie returned home, she told her mother about the secret plan, but first made Amanda promise not to breathe a word of it to Peter. Amanda wasn't so sure this idea was the best way to get Ashley walking again, but Katie argued, "Mom, Ashley wouldn't even try walking if she didn't do it this way. She's too afraid of disappointing her dad."

"Katie, if it gets to be too much, or if you think Ashley needs medical supervision, you are to stop immediately," Amanda instructed firmly.

"Don't worry, Mom. We'll be very, very careful. Robert helped the physical therapist before and knows when Ashley needs to stop or when she's hurting too much."

Katie called Ashley every night that week to check on her progress. Some days Ashley sounded up and happy, while other days she sounded down and discouraged. Katie gently tried to help with kind words. To keep things light, she gossiped about things at school and told funny stories about Emily and her other friends, and even shared Max's latest antics. While she was encouraging, Katie hoped Ashley wouldn't totally obsess about walking again, just in case it didn't work out.

"You can do it, Ashley, don't give up. A few more days and I'll be there to help."

She then launched into the fun things they could do together when Ashley was able to get around on her own, but was careful to include activities they could share if Ashley's wheelchair remained her throne.

Thursday night's conversation started with a surprise. Gushing excitement Ashley exclaimed, "Katie, guess what!" I went down to the stables to see Blaze and she remembered me, even without giving her a sugar cube!"

"That's fantastic!" Katie replied excitedly. Wow, this *was* happening the way she prayed it would. Things were looking good!

Katie went to Ashley's house for as many weekends as she could over the next months. Sometimes she left on Saturday so she could spend more time with Emily. Em told her, "You go, Katie, you're really helping Ashley. Don't worry about me!"

One weekend Ashley suggested Katie bring Emily to visit. The following Saturday and Sunday worked for everybody and Katie was really excited to have Em meet her new friend.

Bright and early on Saturday, Robert again parked the shiny limo in front of the Richards' apartment building. But this time Katie would have company in the big back seat. After enjoying a cup of coffee and Danish with Amanda, Robert loaded the girls into the car and soon the trio was off to the Hamptons.

The girls quickly chose *Bridesmaids* to pop in the disc player and soon were laughing so hard that Robert lowered the glass partition to make sure nobody was choking. Ashley learned what drinks and snacks Katie loved and made sure the limo was well stocked with her favorites.

Before they knew it, Robert turned into the long driveway leading to the Cummings' estate. As the massive stone house came into view, Emily whispered, "Unreal, absolutely unreal! No wonder you love coming here!"

Ashley was waiting for the girls in her usual spot and welcomed Emily like a long lost friend.

"Come on in! Bertie is waiting with another one of her fab lunches. Pretend you're hungry, even if you snacked all the way here," Ashley laughed. "Bertie has been preparing for days!"

The girls went upstairs as Robert brought their suitcases to the guest suite adjoining Ashley's room. It was decided Em would stay with Katie since the bedroom she enjoyed every weekend she visited offered two queen beds.

Emily's mom insisted on giving a hostess gift to Ashley, as well as small gifts for Bertie and Robert.

Emily, Queen of All Things Trendy, chose a leather wrap bracelet studded with turquoise beads for Ashley. It was fashioned by Chan Luu, the absolute coolest designer. Em didn't miss a thing when it came to the latest fashions.

Immediately Ashley wrapped it around her wrist and all the girls agreed it was totally outrageous.

Bertie was gifted with a red paisley silk scarf and Robert's gift was a silver key ring. They were surprised by the gifts, and loved the special attention. They both thought Ashley's new friends were the best!

As usual, Bertie presented a gourmet lunch, worthy of a five-star restaurant. Knowing most girls love mac and cheese, Bertie took the comfort dish to a new level. Using homemade pasta, she created a thick sauce of sharp cheddar, white cheddar, Gruyere, fontina, and a touch of Swiss to make the ultimate casserole. With a crust of buttered bread crumbs, it was a dish to die for! A tomato, basil and mozzarella salad added a light touch to the meal, while rich cream cheese brownies topped with lush raspberries filled the dessert platter. This casual Saturday lunch was really over the top!

After second helpings of everything on the table, the girls set out for the stables to visit Blaze and give her a carrot or two. Derek, who often helped his dad tend to the horses, was brushing Blaze when they arrived.

Derek was fourteen and drop dead gorgeous. With tousled blonde hair and blue eyes the color of the morning sky, he could knock the socks off of any girl and Emily, Katie and Ashley were no exception. Wearing worn blue jeans and a tight long-sleeved black tee, to which Emily immediately gave her fashion seal of approval, he greeted them with "Hey, Ashley, how's it going?"

"Not bad," she replied with a coy smile. "You haven't met Katie yet, and this is her friend Emily who's visiting for the weekend."

Derek nodded hello to the girls.

"I haven't seen you in awhile," Ashley added, wondering where he had been keeping himself.

"I've been helping out at the Barnett's house doing odds and ends, but I'll be here on the weekends from now on."

The girls glanced at each other and their eyes screamed, "Well, that'll sure make the weekends even more fun!"

Derek had no idea what they were thinking. He was just a good kid helping his dad, but something about these three had him thinking he might be looking forward to his weekends at the Cummings' stable more than he thought he would.

"Gotta go, need anything?"

"No, thanks," they replied in unison and started giggling when Derek was out of earshot.

Emily was the first to regain her composure and exclaimed, "Wow, is he ever the cutest thang!" Still laughing, Katie and Emily started pestering Ashley for details about her stable help, but she just told them they'd have to find out for themselves.

Hearing snorts and whinnies coming from the far stall, the three clomped and wheeled through the stable to visit Ashley's pride and joy, the beautiful Blaze.

Blaze loved people, especially friends of her young mistress. As soon as the horse caught a whiff of Ashley, her deep pink tongue began long licking motions—Blaze loved to give kisses! Being city girls, Katie and Em were a little afraid of the large horse, but before long they were petting the mare and treating her to raw carrots.

Ashley had a few sugar cubes hidden deep in her pocket, but Blaze knew exactly where they were. The city girls almost rolled in the hay from laughing so hard when Blaze wouldn't stop nudging Ashley's coat pocket to get at the sweet treat. Blaze put on quite a show that afternoon!

They spent the rest of the day in Ashley's bedroom gossiping about boys, fashions, and movie stars while munching on treats Bertie sent up almost hourly. Finally Emily could stand it no longer and asked to see the clothes closet Katie had described so vividly.

Standing in the doorway to what could only be described as the entryway to fashionista heaven, Em was freaked by the racks of outfits marching before her on the automated poles.

Every outfit was hung with its matching accessories, but Emily was soon pulling one skirt to go with a top from another rack to create fun new looks for Ashley. Her eye for style was amazing and the two other girls called Emily "the one-woman runway wonder." She could certainly be a future host for *Dress for Less*.

Ashley called Bertie to come up to watch Emily in action. The gentle housekeeper was amazed at this thirteen-year-old girl's exceptional talent and tried to jot down as many outfit combinations as she could, knowing there was no way she would remember to combine the colors and prints Em did so effortlessly.

As the day wore on, there was no doubt about it. The three girls had forged a team with an attitude that screamed, "C'mon world, bring it on!" In just a few hours, strong bonds were formed that would last a lifetime.

Before dinner, the trio went to the gym so Ashley could work her therapeutic exercises with Robert's help. Emily and Katie sat on the sidelines cheering her on as she went through her series of routines. Katie was pleasantly surprised at how flexible Ashley had become since she last saw her work out. The determination on Ashley's face spoke volumes. She was going to walk again, no doubt about it. It was still a painful process for her, but Ashley had learned to visualize her success and that kept her going.

That evening as they were sitting around the fireplace in the living room armed with cupcakes and hot chocolate, the three discussed their dreams. Of course Em wanted to be a fashion designer, but also saw herself as a writer. Ashley wanted to own her own antique store, possibly remembering the connection the beautiful old treasures had created between her and her mom. Katie had the most serious ambition of all. She wanted to become a doctor and save people's lives.

Deep down they knew they would probably change their minds a hundred times before they grew up, but that night they shared their hopes and dreams for the future.

Katie and Em couldn't help but ask Ashley what it was like being the daughter of a famous star. While there were obviously a zillion perks, it couldn't be easy or wonderful all the time.

Ashley sighed and told them how sometimes she wished Peter was just a plain old dad. But then again, he was always there when she needed him, no matter what. She missed him when they were apart, but said she was happy he'd been coming home from the west coast more now that he seemed interested in Katie's mom.

Peter was still filming, but surprised Amanda on several weekends when he flew home unexpectedly. They were becoming a couple, but Katie and Ashley were so wrapped up in their growing friendship, they hadn't really noticed what was happening between their parents.

Katie shared her life and how it wasn't easy for her and her mom sometimes, but that she too wouldn't want a life any different. She had a mother she adored, and that made up for a lot she didn't have materially.

Emily had the easiest life of all, the girls decided, or so they thought. But Em's parents fought a lot at home. This was something she didn't tell anyone, but pushed deep into that little corner of her mind where she kept the things she wanted to forget. She hated the nights she would hear her mom accusing her dad of being with another woman.

Hiding under her covers, Emily would put her fingers in her ears so she couldn't hear the harsh words they hurled at each other. As much as she wanted to talk about how the arguing scared her, she just couldn't tell her friends, not tonight.

CHAPTER FOURTEEN

Gobs of Gossip

The press was getting wind of a romantic relationship brewing in the life of Peter Cummings.

While at his home in the Hamptons, he was caught on tape with a beautiful woman holding his arm as he walked around town. As the paparazzi do so well, they quickly identified the woman as one Amanda Richards. But, detailed information about this mystery woman didn't appear anywhere they hunted in the States, so their Google searches expanded to Europe.

Ashley Cummings had been spotted about a block behind her father with a teenage girl pushing her wheelchair. Photographers assumed the girl was hired help so she was ignored as they snapped photos of "sad, crippled Ashley."

Relentlessly the scandal sheet reporters followed Peter around Hollywood and shouted questions about his love life whenever they could corner him. Peter just ignored the hounding, which only increased the frenzy.

One Sunday afternoon, Ashley was spotted at East Hampton with the same girl pushing her wheelchair. It became apparent the girls were friends and one photographer noted how much the girl resembled Amanda Richards. The hunt was on!

Amanda reportedly had been seen shopping in Soho and media vultures quickly descended on the city. Finally they found her, working in a neighborhood diner! How could this be?

The girl attending to Ashley had been spotted leaving a junior high school and after quizzing students, reporters identified her as Katie Richards, Amanda's twelve-year-old daughter. School security officers were put on high alert as paparazzi swarmed the school grounds jockeying for a photo of Katie.

The madness became manic!

Amanda felt like a deer caught in a car's headlights. Everywhere she turned, flashes exploded in her face and questions were screamed at her. Sometimes it scared her when reporters jostled the crowd around her. This was not fun!

Her boss was excited about all the new customers pouring through his door because of the publicity, but he was also worried about Amanda and how the sudden fame was affecting her. He saw Amanda smiling and acting her usual pleasant self, even when being harassed with dozens of questions. It couldn't be easy for her.

Amanda knew her life was forever changing. She discussed the sudden attention with Peter and he hoped she could handle it. This was not what he wanted to happen.

Peter was used to the relentless hounding. Over the years, hundreds of articles with tantalizing headlines had been written about him. Stories sensationalizing Anne's death and Ashley's accident had been the most difficult to handle. He knew reporters and photographers had to make a living so he tried to be generous with interviews, but when lies were told or his words twisted, Peter got angry.

Most of all he wanted to protect Ashley from the glare of the outside world. She simply didn't deserve the ceaseless attention that could make her life more difficult.

It hurt him when Amanda's situation was exploited. Headlines ranging from *Poor Girl, Rich Girl, Rags to Riches* to *Money Hungry Honey* tore him apart. He knew headlines sold magazines and tried to explain this to Amanda. He asked her to ignore the magazines' blaring headlines at the supermarket check-out.

He didn't have to worry. Amanda had been through so much in her life she felt she could handle just about anything.

As Peter did about Ashley, Amanda worried more about her daughter than herself.

Peter and his agent called Katie and talked with her about handling the press. After that conversation, Amanda and Katie tried to go about their everyday lives, armed with Peter's valuable suggestions.

The hardest part for Katie really didn't involve the pestering press. Instead, she was confused by what was happening at school.

Everyone now wanted to be Katie's best friend—the nice kids, bullies, jocks, and even the teachers wanted to boast they knew the girl in the spotlight. Katie tried to be nice to everybody, but it was all so smothering for her. She used to envy the lives movie stars led, but now realized the other side of fame.

Katie wished she could talk with Angelina again, but she was never in the shop when she stopped by after school. She was surprised Angelina didn't leave a note on the door for her customers. Angelina always knew the right thing to say and offered words of comfort when Katie needed them the most. Instead of a heart-to-heart talk, Katie could only rub her little locket, close her eyes, and let Angelina's words warm her.

She remembered so well when Angelina warned, "Stay true to yourself, my dear. Life has many ups and downs, nothing is ever perfect. We all face challenges but I know you will conquer them all."

It was so funny how this strange little woman with the sweet pixie face and twinkling eyes had such an effect on her. What was happening to her?

———————

After weeks away from home, Peter finally finished the movie he was filming. He couldn't wait to get home to see Ashley, Amanda and Katie. He'd never been away from his daughter for so long, but she seemed to be thriving with Katie's attention.

CHAPTER FIFTEEN

Hugs and Kisses

Peter called Amanda the very night he arrived home from Los Angeles. Katie answered the phone and knew exactly who it was when Peter said, "Hi, Katie. Is your mom at home? It's Peter, Ashley's dad." Katie called her mom and teased, "Guess who's on the phone? Do you want to talk with a movie star?"

Amanda grinned and waved her daughter from the room.

"Amanda, I would love to spend next Sunday with you. I can be in the city all day and there's not one thing I have to do. Katie will be here with Ashley and we deserve a little time to ourselves. What do you think? Will Herb give you the day off?"

"I can ask him, but I can't promise anything. It's been very busy since we have so many more customers because I'm so famous now," she teased.

"Well, beg, plead, and carry on if you have too," Peter joked back.

Amanda said she'd let him know the next day. Her answer, of course, was yes. Herb was a sweetheart.

Their day in New York started with breakfast at the Cozy Corner where Amanda was waited on for a change. Peter left a very generous tip and signed autographs for the dozens crowding the diner until his fingers crunched.

A cab ride took the two to Fifth Avenue where they walked the street enjoying the department stores' display windows. The Saks Fifth Avenue store windows were filled with magnificent clothing from decades past. The vintage look was taking over the fashion scene.

Amanda excitedly said, "It looks like Katie's friend Emily really called it. Em loves fashion and said about a year ago that vintage clothing was going to be the next big thing. She went to all the consignment stores and bought skirts, sweaters, handbags and hats when they were really cheap. Now she's selling them back to the same stores for three times what she paid. That girl really has an eye for trends."

After passing a few displays, Amanda commented, "Looking at the windows is like we're actually in somebody's closet or attic. These old clothes are really something."

"Let's go in and shop, Amanda. Please let me buy you something special."

"Peter, I'm just happy to look in the windows and really, I don't need a thing."

They stopped on a corner and bought two salted pretzels from a vendor and loaded them with mustard. Continuing along, they soon found themselves standing in front of the Tiffany windows. Amanda was in heaven looking at the elegant blue boxes piled high in the displays.

Heads started turning as people recognized Peter and asked for autographs. Peter knew once spotted, the paparazzi wouldn't be far behind, especially since the mysterious woman was on his arm.

He had to act quickly and spied an extravagant diamond bracelet draped on black velvet in the window. He told Amanda he wanted to buy it for her right then, but again she insisted she didn't want anything.

Boy, he thought, I've never met a woman like this before.

Hailing a cab to get out of the spotlight, Peter took Amanda to his favorite restaurant tucked inside the Plaza Hotel. Since

Peter was a favored regular, they were seated immediately near the back so no one would bother them.

The staff was delighted to see Peter again.

"Hi, Mr. Cummings, so glad you're back!" Amanda heard these words countless times as they were led to their table. Once seated, Peter ordered a bottle of champagne.

He had something special to say and champagne would be a perfect way to start the conversation. As the waiter poured their glasses of bubbly, then silently backed away, Peter turned to Amanda and whispered, "I'm falling madly in love with you. What do you think about that?"

"Oh, Peter, for so long I dreamed of meeting someone special, and then I gave up hoping since life just took over. I am falling in love with you, too. But we have so much to consider before our relationship can continue any further. Do you think our girls will accept us being together?" This was Amanda's greatest concern.

"Amanda, we are two adults," Peter began. "Life is so short, as you and I both know. The girls seem to get along very well. I believe given time, they will be thrilled that you and I are once again happy."

"I love Katie already, and both girls know they will always be precious to us both. What are we waiting for?"

Amanda could not believe this was happening to her, but already knew there would never be any one but Peter for her. It really had been love at first sight for both of them. Right out of a movie script! She prayed Katie would accept that her mother was falling in love and wanted to share her life with Peter. It had been just the two of them for so long and it worried her that Katie might feel abandoned. She worried about Ashley too. There was just so much to think about!

Amanda and Peter left the restaurant hand in hand and very much in love. They took a horse and buggy ride through Central Park where they discussed what tomorrow would bring, and possibly the years to come. After a while the buggy returned them to the Plaza.

Robert soon pulled up to drive Amanda home and take Peter to the Hamptons. He could tell by their expressions that something serious was going on.

When they were alone in the limo, Robert asked, "And how was your day, Mr. Cummings?"

"Well, Robert, I think I found a gem, and it's not the emerald!"

With that comment, Peter laughed like a young boy in love.

CHAPTER SIXTEEN

A Big Step

Robert had dropped Katie off before he picked up her mother and Peter at the hotel. When Amanda came through the apartment door, Katie looked up and was surprised how radiant her mom looked. She was wearing her ivory suit accented with a burgundy silk blouse which Katie knew her mom wore only for special occasions.

"Mom, where in the world have you been?"

Looking serious, probably enough to scare Katie half to death, Amanda asked her daughter to sit down because she had something important to discuss with her.

Katie couldn't imagine what it could be, but was concerned because this was so unlike her mother.

Did she lose her job, or was she sick? No, she looked too good to be sick, Katie thought. She took a seat and cuddled Max on her lap to brace herself for what was to come.

"Katie, "Amanda began hesitantly. "Something has happened that may change our lives, but I want you to be part of any decision. Let me say you are number one in my life, you always have been and always will be."

"Mom, you're scaring me! What is it?"

"Well, this happened very fast, but I have fallen in love with Peter and he loves me too. We want you girls to know what's been happening and want to know what you think about all this. After all, our relationship will affect your lives."

Katie was overwhelmed at the news, but was thrilled too. She really liked Peter, and as far as Ashley went, well, they were like sisters now.

"Does Ashley know?"

"No, she doesn't. Peter didn't want to say anything until he asked me if I wanted to be part of his life. If I said I wasn't interested in continuing our relationship, he didn't want to mention it to her. Peter knows Ashley had a very difficult time after her mother died.

"You know Katie, if Peter asks me to marry him I'll say yes, unless you have very strong feelings about our marriage. I know it will mean a big change for us, moving being the least of our worries."

"Mom, I really like Peter and I want you to be happy. I'm really excited for you, but I don't know if Ashley will freak. I have no clue how she would feel about all this. She talks about her mom a lot, but also wants her dad to be happy again."

"Katie, I can't replace her mom and I would never try to do that, but I would be there for her always, just like I am for you."

With that, Katie gave her mother a big hug. They would wait to hear the reaction Peter sensed when he told his daughter about his growing feelings for Amanda. Amanda prayed Ashley would echo those of her own daughter. She wanted things to work out so much!

<hr />

Katie spent the next weekend at the Cummings' house. Peter had social events to attend so the coast was clear to visit the therapy rooms. For weeks they had been working on motion exercises, but Robert felt Ashley was now ready to try the walking bars.

Katie couldn't tell if Peter had talked with Ashley about her mom. She didn't think so because Ashley seemed just the same. Katie worried if Ashley didn't like the idea of a stepmom, she might stop trying to walk as a defense to keep things as they were between her dad and herself.

After all, Katie lost her father when she was very young and Ashley's loss was much more recent. Katie had no real history with her father so there was nothing to replace, but Ashley had loved her mother for years and had a heart full of memories.

Robert's voice interrupted Katie's thoughts.

"Well, Ashley, how do you feel about trying to walk holding the rail? I'll be supporting you all the way."

"Robert," she replied nervously. "I'll try, but yes, please stay right next to me. I'm so afraid I'll fall."

When Robert first rested Ashley's arms on the side rails, she collapsed to the floor and started to cry.

"I can't do it, I just can't do it," she sobbed.

"Oh, yes, you can, Ashley. It will just take more time. No one ever said learning to walk was easy. Remember, when you were a baby, you took one step at a time and fell down hundreds of times."

Robert lifted her to the rails again.

"Now concentrate, Ashley, one step, just one step. This is not a race."

Ashley waited still as a statue for a few minutes and seemed to be focusing on a spot high on the wall. Katie and Robert didn't move a muscle while they waited to see what she would do. Minutes ticked by, and then Ashley put her left foot forward and her right foot followed. It was painful, but she had actually taken two steps!

Yes, she was exhausted from the effort, but she had walked! Katie and Robert cheered, "You did it, Ashley, you did it! Nothing can stop you now!"

With tears streaming down her face, Ashley answered in a soft voice, "If only my mom could see me now."

It was only a beginning, and they all knew it, but it was a big start and had given them hope.

It was time to call it a day. They went upstairs to celebrate Ashley's triumph with a piece of the chocolate cake Bertie had baked that morning. Ashley Cummings would walk again; it was just a matter of time now.

With all the excitement over the last few weeks, Katie hadn't had the chance to talk with Angelina about how her life had changed so much. As soon as she was home again, she would pay a visit to *Miracles Can Happen*. She planned to have a long chat with Angelina that Monday after school.

CHAPTER SEVENTEEN

Poof!

After the school bell rang, Katie started her walk to the little boutique. She would let Angelina in on her mom's secret. If Amanda and Peter did get married, Angelina should expect an invitation to the wedding. After all, she was the one who started it all.

As she rounded the corner, Katie stopped dead in her tracks. The windows once so colorful now stood bare and empty! What had happened?

On the front window hung the original For Rent sign and it looked like it had been there for awhile. Had she been dreaming? How could the store disappear so quickly? Where did Angelina go?

Katie's heart broke when she thought about never seeing or hearing from Angelina again. She ran all the way home and called her mom at work.

Herb answered on the first ring, "Cozy Corner, are you placing an order?"

"Can I speak to my mom, please, is she busy?"

"Katie, is everything okay?"

"Yes, Uncle Herb, everything is fine, I think, but I need to talk with my mom. Thanks."

"Let me get her for you right away."

"Hi, Katie, darling. What's up?"

"Mom, it's so strange. The *Miracles* store and Angelina are gone!"

"What do you mean 'gone?' Is she closed for the day? Perhaps Angelina Angelina took the day off."

"No, she's gone, totally gone. The store is completely empty."

"I can't imagine what's going on. I thought her business was going very well. I hope she's not sick or anything like that. It's strange she never said good-bye. Well, perhaps an emergency came up. When I have a chance, maybe we can find the real estate agent for the building and see what happened."

Amanda tried to make Katie feel better since she knew how much she adored the little old lady who had made such a difference in her life.

"Okay, I guess that's all we can do. Go back to work, Mom. Love you!"

They both hung up with unanswered questions whirling in their minds.

Later that week a letter arrived for Katie Richards addressed in a spidery, but beautiful scrawl. She carefully opened the letter, never dreaming who had sent it to her.

> *Dear Katie,*
>
> *I am so sorry I didn't get a chance to say goodbye. I had to leave very quickly as something came up that needed my immediate attention. Please know I am thinking of you and your lovely mother.*
>
> *I am sure everything is going well for you both. I hope you are enjoying your necklace and will always remember the wonderful talks we had. Always know you are in my heart and hopefully I will see you again.*
>
> *Oh by the way, one of my dear friends owns a little shop called* The Painted Horse *not too far from*

Ashley's home. It's full of lovely antiques and fun finds you might enjoy discovering.
If you ever drop in, tell my friend I said hello.
Take good care of yourself, my dear.

With love,
Your Angelina

Katie read the letter again and looked for a return address, but there was none. She made a note of Angelina's friend's shop. Maybe Robert would take her there and she could find out where Angelina had gone. Certainly her friend must know something. Why didn't Angelina tell her his name?

CHAPTER EIGHTEEN

Forever and Ever

Katie didn't say a word to Ashley about the romance growing between their respective parents. She didn't like keeping a secret so big, but she knew Peter would tell Ashley when the time was right. Katie still had no idea how Ashley would react to the news.

Peter had been watching Ashley grow happier and more outgoing over the past months and was thrilled to see the change in his daughter. He had been worried she was falling into a deep depression the weeks before Katie sent that all important letter about the ring.

But Peter was now worried if he talked about Amanda and Katie becoming a bigger part of their life together, Ashley might become upset. With the holidays approaching, he knew he had to tell her about his plans to ask Amanda to marry him. He planned to pop the question on Thanksgiving Eve. Time was growing short and he didn't want Ashley to hear about the proposal from another source. Fan magazines blasted headlines about Peter's love life all the time and speculation about Amanda was running rampant. Ashley knew the magazines stretched the truth, but some of the stories were hitting very close to home.

Nervous as he was, Peter decided that tonight would be a good time to have his chat with Ashley. Bertie and Robert were off for the night and he and Ashley planned to have a pizza delivered.

Ashley shouted, "Dad, they're buzzing at the gate, Luigi's is here."

"I've got it. Meet you at the kitchen table."

"Perfect!" Ashley loved the nights when she had her dad all to herself. She had no idea the bomb he was going to drop in her lap!

As the two shared the mushroom and pepperoni pizza, Peter steadied himself to give his prepared speech. Whew, he thought, this was much harder than acting ever was!

"Sweetheart, there's something I want to talk to you about."

Ashley replied nonchalantly "Go ahead, Dad, I'm listening." Ashley knew her dad usually started conversations about long months away from home like this and she expected to hear him say he would be shooting a movie in Timbuktu or someplace like that.

"First let me ask you this. What do you think of Amanda and Katie?"

"I absolutely adore them both, but why are you asking? Did something happen to them?" Suddenly fear and anxiety filled Ashley's head.

"No, they're fine. I just wanted to make sure we're both on the same page because I adore them too."

"Dad, I think you're trying to tell me something. Spit it out."

"Ashley, I know your mom can never be replaced and please always know I will never love anyone as I loved her. But I've been so lonely sometimes and I find Amanda is wonderful company for me. I don't ever want her out of my life and I would like to ask her to marry me. But Ashley, if you don't think it would work for all of us, I won't. You are my number one girl!"

Ashley grabbed her dad's hand and started firing one question after another: "Does Amanda know how you feel? Does Katie know? Will we have to move? Will Katie and I be sisters?"

Peter took each question one at a time.

"Yes, Amanda knows how I feel and she feels the same way I do. She talked to Katie like I'm talking to you. You both mean so much to us and we felt you should be included in such a big decision.

"Amanda has talked to Katie already, who by the way is very excited about the whole thing, but she asked Katie to keep it to herself until I could talk with you first. Katie's very worried you won't like the whole marriage idea since the two of you have apparently never discussed this possibility. I'm surprised you didn't see how Amanda and I were getting closer, but I guess kids never think of their parents like that!

"To answer another question, Amanda and Katie will live here and Katie can have the room next to yours if you'd like. Yes, you and Katie would be sisters, you practically are already!

"Amanda loves you very much, and knows Anne was and will always be your mom. But Amanda will be there for you and will help you any way she can."

It took two seconds for Ashley to start asking more questions. "When will you get married? And what kind of wedding will we all have? I'm really happy and so excited for you and for me too! Can I call Katie right away?"

"I'll tell you what," Peter began, "I'll call Amanda and we'll get Katie on the extension and talk to them both. This will be one of the greatest Thanksgivings ever! We all have so much to be thankful for. Now, let's hope Amanda says yes to my proposal. I'm going to surprise her with a ring at Thanksgiving and hopefully we can get married over the Christmas holidays when you girls are out of school.

"Katie can transfer at the beginning of the new semester in January and go with you to Hampton Academy. From what Amanda says, she has the grades to get in. What do you think?"

"I think Amanda better say yes, that's what I think!" Ashley said with a giggle. Deep in her heart she knew her life would change dramatically, but it would be for the best. She loved

Amanda and now her best friend would be her sister. What more could she ask for?

Peter picked up the phone and asked Amanda to marry him, right in front of the girls! Why wait until Thanksgiving? It might not have been the most romantic proposal on record, but it was one of the happiest. Tears flowed from four sets of beautiful eyes, but they were tears of joy celebrating the beginning of new love and adventures to come.

CHAPTER NINETEEN

Bring on the Drumsticks

Thanksgiving dinner turned out to be an elaborate feast. Amanda was able to get time off from work for the holiday. Herb knew it was just a matter of time before he would lose his favorite waitress, but he was happy for her. Amanda had helped build his business with her sunny smile. He'd miss her terribly, but what a wonderful new life she and Katie would have.

Bertie had been busy in the kitchen for days, with Robert offering to taste test everything coming out of the oven. What a guy!

On the big day, the 25-pound turkey slid into the oven early. String beans were cut and the sweet potato pie was latticed to perfection. A mushroom casserole was made with four different kinds of umbrella-shaped morsels filling the dish. A cranberry and mandarin orange compote sparkled in a cut glass bowl while the aroma of yeast rolls and cornbread drifted through the house.

Bertie used favorite recipes from both Peter and Amanda's families for the feast. This was going to be one very special day, she would make sure of that.

When the appointed dinner hour was close, the big silver platter was readied to receive Tom Turkey. It was garnished with red and green grapes, orange slices, and small red berries, and was almost too heavy to carry.

Moss green candles in gleaming silver candelabras were lit and a beautiful centerpiece of yellow, burgundy and white chrysanthemums overflowed in a wicker cornucopia. As a surprise for the girls, Peter and Amanda found crafts Katie and Ashley had made in elementary school to celebrate Thanksgiving. A parade of pilgrims, Indians and teepees marched down the center of the table.

Peter was called to the kitchen to carve the turkey before it was placed on the silver platter. Years before he had played a surgeon in a movie and learned the fine art of carving bodies from a team of script-consulting doctors. He found their detailed instructions worked well for turkeys, too. Peter chuckled when he remembered all the tips they had shared with him. Who said acting wasn't a practical job?

Peter bought gifts for everybody and each carried a handwritten card telling that person how thankful he was to have them in his life.

Katie and Ashley received the latest Tiffany lock bracelets and proudly added them to their wrists. Peter then surprised them with the latest Justin Beiber CD which wasn't going to be released until right before Christmas. It took great restraint to keep the two from rushing to Ashley's room to play it a hundred times.

Bertie was presented with a bottle of Chanel No. 5, her favorite perfume, although Peter much preferred aromas from her kitchen. Robert was given a pair of suede gloves lined with lambskin so he'd be ready for the cold months ahead.

Amanda couldn't imagine what was in her box—it was just huge. She opened it to find another box inside, and then another and another and another. This was like opening Russian dolls!

The last box was small, blue, and tied with a silver bow. She thought of the diamond bracelet Peter wanted to buy her at Tiffany's and suspected that's what it was.

She slowly raised the lid and started to cry. Inside was a round diamond, a ring sparkling so brightly it nearly blinded her.

The large diamond was surrounded by diamond and sapphire baguettes circling the band.

Before Peter could say a word, Amanda murmured "Yes, oh yes!" Peter had asked her to marry him weeks before, but this was a real surprise. She assumed a wedding ring would be the only one she would receive.

The girls started screaming at the same pitch they used for rock concerts. Bertie rushed to get champagne while Robert pumped his fist and cried, "Jolly good!" in his finest London accent.

Peter's eyes held tears when he realized how wonderful his life was to become. Amanda just couldn't stop staring at the third finger of her left hand where Peter finally placed the ring.

With a sob choking her voice Amanda whispered, "I'm so thankful for all of you, my family."

Dessert, tiny pumpkin pies served with clotted cream, was placed at each setting. Plates of almond and chocolate chip cookies and a large bowl of orange and yellow M&Ms were set in the center of the table with pilgrims and Indians standing guard.

It was a Thanksgiving they would talk about for a long time, and food wouldn't be the main topic of conversation, if it was mentioned at all.

After dinner the conversation was consumed with wedding details. When and where would it be, and who would be invited to the big event?

All agreed, January 1 would be the perfect wedding day. It would signify the beginning of the New Year and a new life for all of them.

The Cummings' mansion would be the site and white tents would be erected on the south lawn. They knew snow and cold winds were a strong probability so plenty of heaters and snow blowers would have to be ordered.

Amanda had always loved winter weddings and began to imagine clusters of crystals, silver feathers and draped pearls filling the tents. Of course an ice sculpture would be the centerpiece at the appetizer buffet table and Amanda started thinking of what it should represent.

Time was so short and this was such a busy time of the year! Invitations would have to go out immediately and the guest list started. There was so much to do!

This was one time Peter was glad he was a movie star. He was able to wish things to happen and they magically did. It was time to call in all his favors, that was a given.

By the end of the Thanksgiving holiday weekend, the press knew about Peter and Amanda's engagement and headlines screamed from every supermarket tabloid. Peter Cummings, the most eligible bachelor in the country, was officially off the market. Hearts were broken nationwide, but most were thrilled this beautiful man had found happiness again.

What to wear! Amanda knew exactly what she wanted—she just had to find it. She loved the look of ivory velvet trimmed with white fur and pearls, but had no idea where to look for such a gown. This is when Peter's movie star status was first helpful—Hollywood stylists found exactly what Amanda wanted and a team of seamstresses was dispatched to the Hamptons for fittings.

Amanda's only attendants would be the two soon-to-be sisters, each was declared a maid-of-honor. Katie and Ashley decided to wear the same dress style, but in different colors. They chose velvet to compliment Amanda's gown, and Katie's dress would be a deep cobalt blue while Ashley would wear the dress in a rich deep emerald. Somehow, it seemed only right that emeralds would be important on this day of days.

White roses were ordered by the hundreds. Amanda's bridal bouquet would be a cascading mass of roses with a single white orchid nestled in the center. When she married Katie's dad, her bouquet was created of delicate orchids and she wanted to honor his memory. She knew her first love was looking down and smiling on her happiness.

The girls wanted to carry deep red roses so bouquets were designed especially for them. Since both loved glitter and glamour, both chose to wear feathered rhinestone clips in their hair.

Max, what to do about Max? At first Katie and Ashley thought the regal feline could be included in the wedding party. But after trying to catch Max one afternoon so he could try on a silk top hat they found in a pet store, they gave up on that idea. Max would be invited to live at the mansion, but Katie was going to give him a stern talking-to first. The calico cat didn't have the best manners in the world and his disposition could be downright ugly. But, Katie loved him just the same.

When she wheeled down the aisle with Katie, Ashley would wear her mother's emerald ring to honor her memory. She knew her mom wanted Peter to find love again and would be pleased with his choice of Amanda. The day would be bittersweet for the young girl confined to a wheelchair, but it was the first day of the rest of her life. Ashley felt so lucky to have the gift of a second mom to love her.

A Hollywood event planner named Monique had called the Monday after Thanksgiving and volunteered to help with the wedding. Within days, an elaborate plan for the tents and decorations was unveiled and the wedding was soon heading way over the top.

Monique shared wonderful ideas to create a snowy fantasy fairyland—tiny white lights suspended from high in the tents would be hidden under layers and layers of fluffy sheer organza to create the illusion of billowy winter clouds, while mounds of tulle covering the tent walls would invite guests to feel as though they were floating free in a gentle snowfall. Elegant crystal chandeliers would give the impression of a silvery winter sunset as hundreds of ivory candles cast their warm glow over every table.

Tall clear vases set on oval mirrors would hold clustered white calla lilies and palm fronds sprayed shimmering silver. Floating votives in small crystal vases would gather on the mirrored bases, reflecting light from every direction. Tiny pearls and rhinestones would be scattered over the table mimicking freshly fallen snowflakes.

The food would be out of the world! Peter insisted Bertie be treated as an honored guest on his wedding day and hired Talk of the Town to prepare the wedding feast. Before the ceremony, guests would nibble on trout-crusted toast points, caviar mounded on new potatoes, tiny onion quiches and cheeses and fruits framed by elaborate carved garnishes. Bottles of champagne in buckets sculpted of ice would complete the winter scene.

After the ceremony, held in an adjoining tent, guests would be ushered to the reception pavilion and handed a flute of champagne with a California strawberry added for a touch of color. Servers dressed in shades of ivory would wander the tent and invite guests to enjoy grilled mushroom quesadillas, red pepper crab cakes, flaky brie bundles, and garden vegetable spring rolls, then invite guests to be seated at round tables for eight.

Tables were to be covered with floor length white satin cloths and overlays of the finest Belgium lace. Plush dining chairs would be draped in white satin with glittery silver bows sashaying the backs. A lush branch of evergreen decorated with tiny silver bells would be centered in each bow.

After warming with a generous bowl of chicken artichoke soup topped with fried onions, guests would be offered a choice of entrees—prime rib, salmon, lobster or quail. For those who couldn't possibly decide, they could have them all! Roasted vegetables, garlic smashed potatoes, and baby spinach salad would complete the elegant meal.

Peter couldn't just do without Bertie's signature yeast rolls and begged her to share her recipe with the caterer. As her wedding gift to Peter and Amanda, she wrote her cherished recipe on white vellum in flowery calligraphy and delivered it to Peter and Amanda on a red velvet pillow. What a show stopping gift!

The wedding cake. Ah, what a vision it would be! Peter's good friend Alex, who happened to be a famous pastry chef in Dallas, would be flown to the Hamptons to turn Bertie's kitchen into a whirlwind of flour, sugar and frothy egg whites.

The cake would reach five layers tall and each layer would feature a different cake. The chocolate, yellow pound, carrot, coconut and red velvet layers would be highlighted with dark chocolate ganache, blueberry crème, cream cheese mousse, thick raspberry preserves and rich vanilla custard. A hodgepodge of absolute perfection!

The cake would be iced in white marzipan with edible silver snowflakes falling gracefully as the layers sloped. Perched high on the crowning layer, a silver-framed photograph of Peter, Amanda, Ashley and Katie would proclaim the joyous joining of two families into one.

Oh, how the four agonized over the guest list! That was the biggest worry of all. Because so many already had plans for the holidays, Peter and Amanda decided to keep their wedding very small. Only eighty guests would be invited, and only their closest friends.

Both Amanda and Peter had no living siblings and over the years learned to embrace friends as family. Over the years they learned to embrace friends as family. Now Peter and Amanda could create their own *real* family! Wasn't life wonderful?

———◦◦◦———

Katie did feel a black cloud hovering over her head as the wedding planning charged forward. She and Emily had been BFF and she worried the distance between them would cause them to grow apart. They had been in school together since kindergarten and now Katie would be going to a private prep school more than one hundred miles away. She wasn't worried about leaving her old friends since she was comfortable making new ones, but Katie did worry about missing Em.

Robert sensed something was bothering Katie and after a few minutes of chatting, heard Emily's name mentioned too many times to think Katie's fretting didn't involve her in some way. He had enjoyed Emily on her trips to the Hamptons and quickly offered to pick her up and take her home anytime she wanted to visit.

Just hearing Robert's offer lightened Katie's heart and she rushed to call Em to tell her a room would always be hers. Everybody was happy again.

———

Adding to the wedding hoopla, Amanda worried about moving from their city apartment to South Hampton, but Peter made the task a no brainer. He hired *Father and Son Movers* to pack up their belongings. Katie and Amanda would not have to do anything but direct the men what to pack or discard.

A few days before Christmas, piles of flattened boxes were delivered to the Richards' apartment along with an army of uniformed men ready to form an assembly line. Tissue wrap, tape, and labels flew as the men filled dozens of boxes. In a matter of hours the whole apartment was packed and ready to roll to the Hamptons.

Poor Max hid under the kitchen table the whole time the movers packed, fearing he would end up in the box with his catnip and toys. He sensed he was going to a new home with the women in his life, and in his simple kitty-cat way, hoped plenty of treats were part of the deal. Little did the feline know, Bertie was about to become his new BFF.

Whatever wasn't going with them to the Hamptons would be given to friends or charity. Amanda knew some of the women she worked with at Cozy Corner were struggling and would love to have what she no longer needed. Because Peter's home was furnished to the max, Amanda was giving her furniture, dishes, and appliances to her friends.

Except for their cherished family heirlooms, only clothing, personal items and beautiful memories held deep in Amanda and Katie's hearts would be making the trip east.

Amanda and Katie shut the door to their home of so many years on December 20. Even knowing what a wonderful life was ahead, it was very hard to say goodbye to the home they loved so much.

Organized by Herb, the ultimate entertainer, friends and neighbors hosted a party the night before the move to say goodbye. It wasn't a forever farewell, but all knew their relationships would be changing, and changing dramatically.

As the party wound down, it was time for Katie to say goodbye to Em, her best friend for so many, many years. The girls knew they would see each other at least once every month and would be texting and e-mailing dozens of times each day, but each also knew things would be different.

Hugging tightly, the tears rolling down their cheeks turned into racking sobs as Katie and Em recognized the painful loss ahead. It was so hard to let go!

Finally Em broke away and exclaimed," By the way, you should wear your silver tee and your black slouch cardigan with those jeans. You would really look cool. And don't forget to add your long silver earrings and black ballet flats."

She was at it again! Tears turned to hysterical giggles as Emily went on and on with her never-ending fashion advice.

The holidays were soon approaching. This year, so much other stuff was happening that the holiday and all its activities had to be carefully scheduled.

Robert, Ashley and Katie spent five days searching over three counties for the perfect tree. It took forever to get it into the house with Bertie following close behind with her broom and dustpan in hand.

The glorious tree now stood in the middle of the living room in all its glory. The tree's forest fragrance battled with the aroma of Bertie's gingerbread men to claim the grand prize for "Most Wonderfully Smelly."

Katie and Ashley sat in the living room enjoying the fading day and talked about wedding details non-stop. As Bertie passed the room, she looked to the heavens and declared, "Thank you, Lord, I'm so happy that Justin character is forgotten for at least a little while."

Amanda had been shopping all day and would be arriving in just a few minutes. Tonight being Christmas Eve, they would all come together to decorate the tree.

After a body-warming chili and cornbread supper, Peter, Amanda, Ashley, Katie, Robert, and Bertie gathered in the living room. Now the fun would begin.

Following the unspoken tree decorating rule, the lights went on first. Hundreds and hundreds of clear mini-lights were needed to load the tree with illumination.

Then white garland was wrapped around the fifteen-foot tree. Once it was adjusted, readjusted, and adjusted yet again, glittery silver balls were carefully hung exactly fifteen inches apart. That took quite awhile since Robert insisted on measuring each placement. Good thing Bertie offered plates of cookies and hot chocolate to give them strength!

Katie and Ashley found silver hearts at the CVS and thought they would be perfect to express all the mushy love that was going on in the house these past weeks. Dozens of silver horses pranced on the branches in honor of Blaze. Tiny silver pine cones and lush silver bows were added as fillers.

Wow—the tree was really cool looking and it would be a perfect addition to all the wedding decorations strung outdoors. Standing back to critique their work, bows were fluffed and ornaments straightened before Robert turned off the room lights and switched on the tree.

The room took on a mystical glow with silver reflecting on every surface. It was simply heavenly and a chorus of oohs and ahhs began. After a few minutes, the girls got a little crazy and started singing *Deck, Deck, Deck the Tree* to the tune of *Row, Row, Row Your Boat,* only to collapse in fits of giggles.

Max was definitely in *his* seventh heaven with all the shiny balls to paw. His cat eyes were focused on one particular globe hung deep in the tree. After stalking the fir and trying to wiggle under its branches, poor Max was given his marching orders and relegated to a position watching from a big armchair.

Ashley was an aspiring photographer and her digital camera was given a work-out as she captured all the action. What a night! When the last cookie was munched, everybody marched off to bed so they'd be ready for Christmas morning.

Everybody was up at dawn—this was just the most exciting day of the year, almost. The wedding did give Christmas some serious competition this particular year.

Amanda and Peter had been up practically half the night wrapping gifts. They finally sauntered down the steps around eight to see eyes of anticipation awaiting their arrival. Bertie set a breakfast buffet of scrambled eggs, waffles, hash browns, sausage, and four kinds of sweet rolls to keep the morning meal easy.

Finally it was time to open the presents after singing a few favorite carols. Keeping with Peter's tradition, Bertie and Robert were given generous checks to use for shopping sprees. The checks were wrapped with silly trinkets that were fun to open.

Robert was given a red cashmere sweater too, and Bertie was gifted a pink chenille robe. Katie and Ashley each got a new Nikon camera since they planned to design an elaborate wedding scrapbook as their gift to their parents.

The girls each got a MacBook Air to encourage studying and dozens of funky outfits were boxed under the tree. As a special gift, Amanda presented Katie and Ashley with diamond stud earrings to wear as her maids of honor. This was turning out to be some Christmas!

It would be hard to top the gift Peter presented to Amanda at the Thanksgiving table, but he did try. A set of Louis Vuitton luggage was rolled out and Amanda gasped when she saw the expensive collection. Riding on top of the LV tote laid a metallic Tory Burch handbag holding an envelope. Inside were two first-class tickets to Paris and a gift certificate for Chanel. This deserved one big long thank you kiss!

As she folded the wrapping papers, Amanda thought of the Christmases she and Katie had spent alone. They were warm, wonderful and very special, but now they were warm, wonderful, very special AND a life filled with new loves and adventures. What a year it had been for them, and it all began with a little lady named Angelina!

Peter was presented with an Italian-crafted leather briefcase and a fine ostrich belt with an intricate silver buckle. Amanda splurged on gifts for the first time in her life. She'd been able to save her tips and salary for the past two months since Peter insisted on paying all her expenses until they were married. And, she did dip into the "reward money," she had to admit.

There was one more gift for Amanda which Ashley insisted they had to go outside into the blustery cold to open. After bundling up and walking to the far end of the drive, Ashley insisted all eyes must be shut tight. Within minutes a deep rumble broke the quiet of the early morning.

"You can open your eyes now," Ashley shouted excitedly.

Pulling up the drive with Peter at the wheel was a spanking new British racing green Jag convertible! Amanda would need a car now that she would be living outside the city, and this was definitely a fine ride. Robert had helped Peter choose the English car, and promised to keep it in primo condition. A big red bow was attached to the hood and Peter absolutely insisted the car had to be green as a reminder of the emerald ring that brought them together.

CHAPTER TWENTY

Mystical Magical and More to Come

The week between Christmas and New Years Day was frantic.

There were so many workers in and out of the Cummings house that Bertie felt she lived in a house with a revolving door. The poor woman had a hard time keeping track of who was doing what or going where. She kept the coffee pot on all the time and baked cookies continually and soon became known as the "hostess with the mostest." Nobody was going hungry on her watch!

Because the time between the engagement and the wedding was so short and Amanda was working at the diner most every day, Peter had hired a wedding planner to keep things running smoothly. Peter made sure the planner asked Amanda for her ideas and input about everything since this was really her special day. But, the only thing Amanda really cared about was Peter and everything else took a far second place to her man.

The house was still decorated for the holidays which added so much to the fun. Peter came home one night to find a gigantic Frosty the Snowman in the front yard with six spotlights aimed at Frosty's frozen smile. His friends from Radio City Music Hall sent it over as the ultimate prop for the occasion.

The two big tents were up and the tables, chairs, and heaters brought in. The final guest list included the Cozy Corner crowd with Herb organizing transportation and logistics for the trip. Emily and her parents would be there along with a few friends of Ashley's from school. Derek and his family were also invited since they were part of the Cummings' extended brood.

From the Hollywood side, Julia Roberts would attend with her husband Danny. Their kids were also invited—this wedding was going to be a true family affair. Peter's business manager and agent along with their families would attend too.

Ryan Seacrest recommended a great local band for the reception. He planned to be there with his fiancée. Nobody regretted to the wedding invitation—this would be *the* party of the year!

Tony Bennett, an old friend of Peter's, was delighted to sing *The Girl I Love* for their first dance as husband and wife. Knowing the press would try to gain access to the wedding, Peter and Amanda agreed to hold a press conference and photo shoot an hour into the reception to keep everybody happy. Peter set up a press tent and stocked it with drinks, snacks, and small favors. No wonder Peter was loved by all, even the paparazzi!

The one thing Amanda forgot to buy was her wedding shoes. She wondered if she should buy boots since the weather could be iffy. Rushing into Saks just two days before the wedding, Amanda splurged on Jimmy Choo sling backs in a pale gold shimmer. So what if her toes froze—these shoes rocked!

Raul was coming from the Hair Affair to fling and sling the tresses of the three ladies of the hour. He was excited the girls were wearing feathers in their hair—he loved the daring challenge of that statement!

Amanda wanted those who had been so nice to her to be part of her special day. She was still Amanda Richards, pure and simple, and that's what Peter had loved about her from the very start.

Peter and Amanda's wedding day dawned with snow falling softly, setting the most beautiful background for a glorious day. Three cheers for the Hamptons' road crews—all roads were clear and dry by the time guests were due to arrive at five o'clock.

As evening fell, twinkling lights, garlands, evergreens, and vases brimming with white roses set a stage that could only be called magical.

Music wafted over the crested snow as guests gathered with champagne in hand. When Peter heard the weather might be snowy, he hired horse-drawn sleighs to carry guests from the parking area to the wedding tent. The children were particularly excited about this little touch, especially since Ashley thought to put a basket of carrots in each sleigh for the kids to feed the horses.

Before Amanda and Katie left the house, they sat and held each other for a long time. No words were spoken, but each knew this was the blessed beginning to a wonderful life for them.

A gentle knock on Amanda's door reminded the mother and daughter that it was time to go. Robert led them to a gold sleigh decked with boughs of white holly and masses of red roses. Ashley was already seated in it, her wheelchair waiting at the wedding tent.

"Amanda, Katie, and Ashley," Robert began, "Peter wanted you to have your own golden carriage, and it's my honor to drive you to the ceremony."

"Wow, mom," Katie whispered. "Don't you feel like Kate Middleton riding to meet her prince?" Katie was always the romantic.

They arrived at the wedding tent and Peter's friends helped them from the carriage. Robert had two roles to play that night—carriage driver and best man. He had to rush to stand with Peter at the end of the aisle to wait for the bride and her maids.

Peter looked exceptionally handsome in an Armani tux with a silk scarf casually thrown over one shoulder. He was ready to marry the woman he loved.

A traditionalist, Amanda wanted to hear the strains of Mendelssohn's *Wedding March* as her two daughters went before her. As all eyes drifted to the back of the tent, Katie and Ashley started down the aisle. Ashley did just fine in her wheelchair as Katie walked beside her.

When they reached Peter, he bent down and hugged them as they kissed him on each cheek. It was impossible to find a dry eye in the tent as Peter looked lovingly at his two girls.

Then the music faded and everyone turned to see the bride. Amanda stood with her arm in Herb's, but her eyes were reaching for Peter. The harpist began to play *All I Ask of You* from *The Phantom of the Opera* as Amanda and Herb started down the long aisle.

Amanda was simply breathtaking. Her golden hair cascaded over the white mink cape she wore over her velvet gown. Peter's wedding gift to her, pearl and diamond drop earrings, accented her beautiful face. From the moment he saw her leave the carriage, Peter could not take his eyes away from the woman he loved so much and brought so much joy into his life.

The couple wrote their own vows and included their daughters in their promises to love and cherish each other. The judge pronounced Peter and Amanda man and wife, everyone applauded while wiping tears away, and then the party started!

Ashley, Katie and Emily sat together in a corner and didn't stop talking about how beautiful the wedding was. Emily was the fashion critic as each guest's gown was dissected and she had the girls in hysterics with her witty commentary.

To the girls' delight, Derek switched place cards and joined their table. He was dressed in a navy double-breasted suit and a French-cuffed shirt, and Emily quickly pronounced him perfectly attired. With tousled hair brushing his collar and an oh-so-wicked grin, Derek just might give Justin a run for his money. The group of three soon became a foursome of three girls and a guy.

The dance floor was moving in waves and several times Amanda and Peter joined their friends on the floor, only to have the dancing stop as the others encouraged them to have one more wedding dance alone. Tony Bennett sang almost every romantic song he knew and dedicated each to the happy couple. *The Way You Look Tonight* was performed at least three times!

The evening was coming to an end. The lead vocalist in the band tapped his mic and asked everyone to take their seats. No one knew what to expect next.

He announced Ashley had requested a special dance with her dad. Peter got up from his table and wheeled Ashley to the center of the dance floor. He started to lift her from her chair, but she quickly admonished, "Wait a minute, Daddy."

A hush fell over the room when Ashley Cummings raised herself out of her chair and walked to her father. Peter, with Amanda and Katie now by his side, started to cry, leading a symphony of sobs from the entire room.

Peter listened carefully as Ashley told him what Katie and Robert had been helping her do.

When he regained his composure, Peter offered, "Ashley, this is the greatest gift any parent could ever receive. What a miracle you've given yourself and me."

When the last guest said goodbye, Amanda asked Katie to take a little walk with her under the winter moon.

"So Katie, what do you think of all this?"

"Mom, I couldn't be happier for you, me, Ashley, and Peter. Who would have ever thought this could happen to us? If it weren't for Angelina . . . Their words drifted off as they looked at the stars twinkling above, and for just an instant, they thought they saw the words *Miracles Can Happen* emblazoned across the dark night sky.

As quickly as it appeared, the vision was gone. Did they see what they thought they did?

Arm in arm, the mother and daughter slowly walked inside to join Peter and Ashley.

A miracle did happen somehow, someway, and deep in their hearts, they knew Angelina would be with them always.

EPILOGUE

It was a warm summer day and Ashley and Katie were in their pjs lying flat on their backs in the middle of the living room deciding what to do for excitement that particular Tuesday. The aroma of bacon frying and French toast baking was teasing them from the direction of the Cummings' kitchen. Bertie was at it again while Robert was in the back watering the rose bushes.

Amanda and Peter were finally in Paris on their honeymoon. They decided to wait for warmer weather to stroll along the Seine—a trip to France in frigid January wasn't going to do it for this pair of newlyweds.

The doorbell rang and Katie jumped to answer. A Fed Ex driver held a letter addressed to both girls. Strange, Katie thought as she showed it to Ashley. A lighthearted game of tug-of-war started as each tried to rip the cardboard envelope open.

"Okay, you read it, Katie, before we destroy the whole thing."

> *Dear Girls,*
> *I am hoping this finds you both happy with your new lives. I have a request of you that would make this little old lady so happy if you could help me. Before I ask, I am truly sorry about leaving New*

York without saying a real good bye. Something came up and I had not a moment to spare.

The good news is, I am now a partner in the store called The Painted Horse. *Remember I wrote you my friend owned it?*

It's not far from where you live. I would simply adore it if you could stop by to see me at your earliest convenience. I have something rather important to talk with you about.

Enclosed are the directions to the store. Perhaps Robert and Bertie can drive you to visit with me.

My very best regards to your parents.

With love,
Your Angelina

The new sisters looked at each other and finally Ashley asked, "What could she want to see us about?"

"I have no idea," Katie answered. "But I think we should go and find out. It sounds very mysterious to me."

"Katie, let's ask Robert if he has the day free and if he would like to spend it driving us around. We could stop at antique stores along the way to *The Painted Horse* and make a day of it."

"Sounds like fun, Ash, let's go see what he says."

Always up for excitement, Robert assured the girls watering the roses could wait until evening. It would be a great excuse to take the Jag convertible for a spin!

The girls threw on jeans and tees and completed their outfits with pairs of jeweled flip flops. While Emily was miles away, her unspoken advice always prompted them to reach for fashionista status. They flew down the stairs and settled in the breakfast room for Bertie's morning's offering.

"Bertie, please take the day off and come join us for an adventure. Robert said we can take the Jag and put the top down. It'll be fun!"

"Sounds good to me. I'll pack a picnic lunch and we can stop at the little lake where the crabby ducks live and enjoy our lunch there."

"Super," they both sang at once, and then burst out laughing just thinking about crabby waddling ducks.

"You two are something else," Bertie said shaking her head.

Katie had a question. "Bertie, can I ask you something?"

"Sure, go ahead, what is it, darlin'?"

"How did you find Angelina in the first place? What made you take Ashley's outfits to that particular store?"

"You know, the whole thing was rather strange. I got a letter in the mail asking if we had any clothes we would like to offer to charity. The letter came from a new consignment store in New York called *Miracles Can Happen* that sold donated clothing and gave the proceeds to the charity of the donor's choice.

"The letter went on to say outfits must include a pair of shoes and purse to complete the look. I thought this was a little pushy myself.

"Crazy as it was, Ashley had tons of things she couldn't wear any longer so we decided to go through her closet and weed out what she no longer liked or was too cumbersome to wear in her wheelchair.

"So I packed several boxes and Robert drove me to the city. It was the day Angelina was opening her little shop, and was she ever busy! I just had time to fill out the forms to give any money to the Make A Wish Foundation and then I was off in a flash to run a few more errands. Angelina was so lovely and I sensed something very unusual about her, but couldn't put my finger on what it was."

"You know, Bertie, I got the same feeling when we first met. I've really grown to like her a lot. Angelina's so interesting and has gobs of stories to tell. But yes, there is something very different about her, like she's from another world."

Ashley laughed at this bizarre conversation. "There you go again with your wild imagination, my new sister!"

They were off before noon, hair flying in the wind. The skies were clear blue with not a cloud in sight as Robert hugged the curves of the ocean. What a great day for an adventure!

Just beyond a wide loop in the road, *The Painted Horse* loomed large. Angelina was framed in the doorway, her arms wide open.

"My dears, I knew you would come. I have so much to tell you!"

Let's see what you think.

What lesson do we learn from Miracles Can Happen?

What could have happened if Katie had kept the ring?

Was Amanda right when she insisted Katie return the ring?

Do you think Angelina has special powers?

How old do you think Angelina is?

What would you have told your child or friend to do with the ring?

How important do you think Bertie is in Ashley's life?

How important do you think Robert is in Ashley's life?

Why do you think Ashley didn't care about walking?

What do you think of buying your clothes at a consignment store?

What do you think happened at the wedding when Katie and her mom looked up in the sky?

Do you think it was just their imagination?

Finally . . . What could Angelina want to see the girls about?

ABOUT THE AUTHOR

It's not enough for Caryn Lesley Blank to enjoy the balmy breezes and laid-back lifestyle of South Florida with her husband, Michael. She has a passion to write, especially for young people who are learning the lessons of life.

Caryn's latest book, *Miracles Can Happen: The Ring,* reaches tweens and teens. Her first book, *The Barnyard Wedding,* was written for the younger set. As a mother of three and grandmother of five, Caryn has experienced all that a houseful of children can offer.

Caryn created a journal, *Treasured Words,* for parents to use to record the wonderful words and delightful comments their children say, often uncensored! Her poem, *Like It Used to Be,* appears in *The Best Poems of 2003.*

"There are always lessons to be learned" is the recurrent message in Caryn's works. Embracing a world filled with kindness is especially important to this wise author, and her words encourage young people to look for the important things in life.

Visit Caryn's blog, *My Thoughts on Life,* at carynlesley@ blogspot.com.